CASSIE LEIGH

until

death

do us

part

Haunted Romance Series,
Book 1

Cover design © Cover Couture

http://www.bookcovercouture.com

Photos © Depositphotos

Formatting by AB Formatting

Sassy Typewriter Press

5001 1st Ave SE

Ste. 105 #243

Cedar Rapids, IA 52402

https://sassy.typewriter.press/

ISBN 978-1-940509-28-0

Version 2.0.0

The veil between life and death will part to bring two souls together…

MILLIE was a lonely spirit with no one but her house to keep her company. That changed the day the handsome new owner of her precious home moved in and said hello. She never thought she would have a chance to fall in love again. Now she is chipping away at her past and turning away from the light she thought she was waiting for. There is just one problem; the love of her afterlife is engaged.

This story is for my mother, Lee Mitchell and my aunt, the incomparable "Nanny" Becky Kennedy. Your love and devotion to our family's history shaped me into the woman and the writer that I am today. I don't know where I would be without your support. This edition is also for my readers. Book people are the best people, and I wish I had space to thank you individually, but I trust you know who you are. Thank you.

acknowledgements

It's hard to believe that the original version of this novella has been in print for two years. If you are reading this, and you purchased the first edition, thank you. I can promise you, I did not do a massive rewrite of the story you loved. What I did do was fix one scene that has always bothered me a little and add the epilogue you all have been asking for. Yes, that's right; I wrote that epilogue for all of you. I heard you loud and clear in all of those reviews and the truth was I wanted one too. Thank you for sticking with me on this journey.

I also need to thank some extraordinary people in my life, starting with my family. I dedicated this to my mom and my aunt, but they are just one part of it. My children are the best five cheerleaders I could ask for, and my husband may not always understand but he tries.

This book would be nothing without my editor Barbara Malmberg. She is more than an editor. She is my best friend and frankly is more like a book coach, coaxing me through all the hard moments where I want to walk away. She is joined by Charlotte Penn Clark, Jolene Buchheit, Dylan Moonfire, and the Noble Pen critique group which saw the early gory stages of this book.

I also owe a special thanks to Anna Crosswell of Cover Couture for the three new beautiful covers for this series. As much as I loved my original, the cover she designed for each book is stunning, and I am honored for them to grace my books.

Finally, I want to thank Mickey, Lori, and Rachel of BF Bookies and North Iowa Book Bash. In life sometimes, you meet people and they just kind of adopt you. These are those people for me. They were among the first of many book people who pulled me through the first bumbling year of my publishing career. I should thank many more. I hope that you know who you are because—thank you.

chapter 1

illie spied the real-estate agent through the rosette window of the attic. She loathed the balding relic that now lumbered up the sidewalk since the day he brought developers to tear down her home. Reason told her she should welcome that fool. He could be bringing potential company into her life. She turned away from the window where she sat perched day in and day out. It made her ache with sadness to see the proud farmhouse that she spent her youth in sit empty, no furniture or voices filling it up. But her feelings were not enough to make her welcome the agent.

Twin metallic clunks from outside broke through the stillness of the morning and sent a fluttering sensation running through Millie's midsection. She paced the dusty pine planks; the prospect of new life carried her nearer the door on each pass. She didn't need to look. It would be better if she kept her distance up here in the attic. Unexplained cold spots and footsteps that had no apparent source tended to scare people away.

When the jingle of keys and muffled voices echoed up the stairs, her curiosity won out. Surely she could get a glimpse of them from the stairs. There was no need to go down.

The front door closed with a thud that reverberated through Millie.

The droning voice of the real-estate agent assaulted her ears. "It's a fixer upper but the neighborhood is quiet, and it's in one of the better school systems."

Millie rushed to the landing and leaned over the carved wooden banister. "Don't you mess this up," she shouted down at the agent, whose heavy footsteps she heard lurking in the front room. "Tell these people what a lovely home this was. I'm sick to the teeth of being alone."

Millie blew out a long breath, a habit that was no longer necessary. Why did she bother, the real-estate agent couldn't hear her. She rubbed her hands along the polished rail. It couldn't hurt to go down and take a peek at who the inept fool brought this time. Millie shifted back and forth on the balls of her feet, unable to hold still. No, they'll come to her. She just needed patience—a commodity she had precious little of, unlike time.

"The more we see, the better I like this house." A man's clear baritone echoed off the bare walls of the kitchen in tandem with the banging of cabinet doors. Millie supposed the man behind it was going through opening and closing them as he considered his purchase.

The potential buyer walked into the entryway, leading a woman by the hand towards the stairs where Millie sat. To the diminutive Millie, he seemed tall and dark. When he glanced up the stairs, sharp blue eyes met her own. Even from this distance, Millie felt captive to the vitality that filled them. Though she knew better, she felt as if there was something in that look just for her, some message she wasn't grasping.

He looked away, back at the woman he came with. The absence of his gaze broke whatever unlikely cord of communion had been strung between him and Millie. He couldn't have seen her, no one ever did. Millie's cheeks tingled, remarkably like blushing, if that had been possible. She raised a hand to her cold cheek. He certainly was the best-looking man that the portly agent had ever brought through her home and closer to Millie's age than most of them.

"Noah, I really don't want something that needs this much work," said the man's companion. "I just wanted to walk in after the wedding to our picture perfect starter home." The woman's blonde ponytail swayed as she shook her head.

The woman wore a modern, soft pink sweater that came down to mid-thigh of her form-fitting denim. Millie looked down at her own shapeless ivory dress. It hung past her white stocking-clad knees. Perhaps Millie could have had a better husband if she had been as attractive.

Noah started up the stairs, hand in hand with his future wife. They must have money, Millie assumed because he appeared as richly dressed as the pretty blonde, with her collared shirt and a pullover sweater. Her working-class husband and father would have called him a well-to-do lawyer's son, or maybe a banker. Definitely not the kind of man Millie was used to being around.

Mindful not to touch the couple as they passed her, Millie scooted out of the way. She made no effort to conceal herself further. The woman looked past Millie into the bathroom, appearing completely unaware of her presence. Noah looked right at Millie. She gasped and then ducked behind an open bedroom door, kneeling down. Her heart racing, she peered through the gap below the hinge. When Noah continued into the first bedroom without comment, Millie sighed in relief and moved back into the hall.

He must have been looking through her. It was silly on her part to continue deluding herself that he could actually see her. Just an over-active imagination brought on by decades of loneliness, she chided herself. Only children ever noticed her and usually only the very young. She took extra care not to frighten the little darlings.

"What do you think of this one for the master, Claire?" Noah asked.

"The closet is so small, and the carpet has to go. It'll kill my allergies, and my asthma will flare up," she whined in reply. Her cheeks sucked in and her mouth pursed in a pretty pout.

"I can fix that," Noah promised. He began to count off the benefits on strong hands that appeared rough and used to work, much to Millie's surprise. "Just think of the possibilities. This house is under budget, and we were only looking for three bedrooms; this house has four. The room adjoining this one could be turned into a master bath and walk-in closet."

His plan sounded lovely to Millie. Someone to care for her home and remake it into a special place again, like it had been before her life had fallen apart.

"I don't want to live in a construction zone." Claire crossed her arms in front of her chest and took a step back. "I want move-in ready."

Millie's jaw dropped, and she drifted up beside Claire. "Be reasonable, not every man offers to do something so monumental, you silly woman. Don't you see how lucky you are?" Millie asked, waving her hands in agitation.

"You'll have that." Noah reached out, resting his hand on Claire's arm. "We have three months until the wedding. All I need is eight weeks."

"I'm listening." Claire looked away as if only humoring him.

He moved in close, his voice lowered to a whisper. "I'll move in and start working. You stay in your place and focus on the wedding. You'll move in when we get back from Hawaii."

Mille held her breath, her hands tented together and covering her mouth as she drifted back into the hall. Was it too much to hope that this seemingly ungrateful woman would accept such a generous offer from her betrothed?

Claire sighed, and her arms dropped to her sides. "Well, I'll get to pick my own finishes. I couldn't do that in a house that's already done, there's that at least."

Millie clapped in excitement and spun happily. Finally, some company.

Noah grinned and grabbed Claire's hand. "I knew you'd see. Let's talk to Bob and put in our offer."

Millie beamed with hope from her spot in the hallway. Noah pulled Claire behind him, striding with purpose to the stairs. Millie stepped back out of the way until her waist pressed against the handrail. Noah returned Millie's smile with genuine warmth and a slight nod, silently offering a hello. He didn't pause as he continued down the stairs, leaving Millie disoriented. Her own smile slipped away. Did he see her after all?

chapter 2

illie's sense of time had slipped away in the decades since her death. Weeks may have passed in the void that was her present circumstance, but it seemed only a matter of days. The real-estate agent hadn't come back with anyone else. Hope and anticipation pressed for control, filling the emptiness of her existence.

She lay on the wide planks of the attic floor glaring at the beam overhead as though it had done something more than hold the rope. She spent most of her time here, pacing the floor or staring out the lone rosette window that overlooked the front lawn. She could go downstairs if she chose, but without another person here to stir her curiosity or fill her isolation with the illusion of one-sided companionship, she preferred to avoid the minefield of memories.

Change had been the only means to mark the passage of

time. She spent the first few decades with steamer trunks and wooden crates as furniture in her self-imposed domain. Those gave way in time, replaced by brown cardboard boxes. After the last owner of her home passed away in her sleep, there had only been emptiness. Mrs. Roosa had gotten a doorway to the other side, but Millie never had.

Slamming doors and male laughter broke through her thoughts, filling up the house below her. "He came back!" Millie shouted in triumph as she raced to the rosette window. She welcomed the horde of friends, boxes, and furniture that poured from the armada of vehicles outside and the end of her solitude they represented.

Eager to see the new owner, she rushed down the stairs and through the attic door to the banister where she first laid hungry eyes on him. Noah crossed the threshold into the entryway, arms straining with the burden he carried. Men, who must have come with him, parted to make way before heading back out the door behind him. Noah stacked the box against the wall and stood surveying the progress all around him. His blue eyes were warm with laughter as he raked his hand through sweaty hair.

This was real; this was happening and not just her hopeful flight of fancy. Millie danced in place, happy for the chaos around her and what it meant. When her spinning came to a stop, she spotted men coming up the stairs with a bed frame. She jumped to the side, managing to avoid their accidental touch. She took another step back to move out of the way for the men who followed with the mattress, but stepped into the path of the first pair of men, unaware of her presence as they came back out the bedroom door.

Millie looked down at her stomach, helpless as the elbow passed through her. She felt the pressure of it like someone pocking her, only magnified. She noticed the hair on his arm stood on end and his skin raised into bumpy-looking gooseflesh. He pulled back, rubbing his arm as if to warm himself.

"Did you feel that?" the man asked his friend.

They flattened themselves against the wall as the mattress went by. "Feel what?"

The first man shook his head. "Never mind."

Millie smoothed her hands down over her stomach, now whole after the unexpected breach. Lifeless objects had substance for her, and with concentration, she might even make them move, but the living were another matter.

Unsettled by the encounter, she retreated to the safety of the attic to wait for this to pass. It was exhilarating to see her home so full once more. She wanted to be in the thick of it, but this experience was a timely reminder not to scare her guests away with the cold spots and unexplained occurrences that she left in her wake. She had frightened off her share of homeowners in the early years after her parents left the house. She had only just gotten her new companions here, and she wanted them to stay.

Millie returned to her window to pass the time, straining to see the couple who would be sharing her home. She found Noah easily enough. He stood out to her as he passed in and out with each new load. Millie expected to see Claire pull up with a cadre of women to feed the men who worked so diligently to fill her home. In Millie's day, that's how it would have been. But no women ever came. Instead, Noah left, returning with pizza and beer to repay his friends while they continued to unload the moving truck.

Millie couldn't fathom what the woman was thinking. Claire's man toiled to give her a nice home, yet she was nowhere to be found. Mille wished that her husband had been so thoughtful. Millie's father, not her husband, provided them a place to live after she had eloped. Her husband had changed into another man after the vows were spoken, tearing down her girlhood dreams of married life.

She banished the melancholy thoughts, sweeping them away like dust under the rug. The sky had grown dark and the house quiet. Millie crept down the stairs, past a maze of boxes in various stages of unpacking to find Noah in the kitchen.

A tower of cardboard stood in one corner, waiting to be unloaded into the original oak cabinets that Millie's father had built for her mother. For the time, it was a large kitchen. She had seven brothers and sisters; her mother needed the workspace. While the essentials remained, other things had changed with the times. The appliances were a putrid shade of avocado, and the chipped white with gold-flecked Formica had been added in the fifties.

"Does it bother you having me move into your home," Noah asked. He put a stack of plates into the open cabinet. "I noticed you hid when we came in with boxes."

Millie looked around. Had Claire come after all? She must be standing behind her. But when Millie spun all the way around, they were alone.

Noah closed the cabinet door and looked directly at her. "What's your name?"

chapter 3

illie fled to the attic in desperate need of the meager comfort she could find, pacing her familiar path. Shaking her hands in front of her, her nerves were unraveling. She couldn't overlook this, not the way she had dismissed the smile and that look. Whatever passed between them had not been a flight of fancy in a moment of her own weakness.

Now he had spoken to her as if he had seen her. No one had ever done that and Lord knew, Millie tried to be heard. With so little effort, this stranger had smiled and asked her a question. She sat against the wall, by the attic window, buried her face in her hands and rocked herself. That's when the memory took her, drawing her into its sticky web.

Millie felt herself move through time, her consciousness pulled back to 1938. She wasn't in the refuge of the attic. The smell of lilacs and baby powder perfumed the air around her, and she squeezed her eyes tight against the dainty floral wallpaper that no longer hung in the room she had been transported to.

The forlorn wail that assailed Millie reminded her there would be no way out of this memory; she had to go through it. Resigned to it, she opened her eyes. Her mother knelt beside the bed, hands clasped together in prayer.

Her shoulders quaked with the force of her tears. "Why'd you take my baby, Lord? Haven't I been good enough? She was a strong girl, but you broke her down so low, she couldn't stand it."

Caught in the memory's spell, Millie rested her cold hands on her mother's slumped shoulders, just as she had done that day. "I'm here, Ma. Look at me. You were good enough; it was me."

Her mother pulled her black shawl tight about her, moaning as a fresh wave of tears overtook her, but she stayed there on the floor unmoved. Millie wrapped her arms around her mother to comfort her. The grieving matron shivered violently.

Millie pressed her lips to her mother's damp cheek then whispered, "Ma, I'm still here beside you. Just turn and look at me. Please don't cry anymore—I won't leave."

Her mother's hand pressed to the spot Millie had kissed, her eyes darting around the room wildly as she dragged herself up off the floor. "Don't taunt me, Lord. You took her, but you let me feel her."

Millie looked around the room, silent tears rolling freely down her own face as she searched for a way to make her mother see, as she had that day they buried her broken physical form. Her gaze rested on the photos lined up on the dresser. She spotted the one of her, dressed all in white, standing in front of the house. Millie reached out and pushed the picture slowly across the dresser. Rather than take the sign for what it was, her mother screamed and ran from the room.

With the bedroom empty and her mother's continued despair echoing down the hall, Millie felt the familiar rage rise within her. Where had this strength been while she was living, when it might have aided her? But no, she'd been a coward, hadn't she. Reaching out, she swept the frames off the dresser and screamed out her rage. No one would hear it anyway.

chapter 4

Noah made his way up the attic stairs, careful to tread softly. He hadn't meant to startle her. He had been aware of her that first day while they toured the house. Of course, it was difficult not to be conscious of her when she screamed at their real-estate agent. It was also hard not to laugh. When she started arguing with Claire to buy the house, he knew that it would be safe for them here. She seemed to crave the company.

Now he stood, watching her. She sat with her back to the far wall, hugging her knees to her chest. Her arms wrapped around her head, she rocked back and forth like a frightened child, hiding from a nightmare.

"I didn't mean to scare you. I'm sorry." He held his position at the top of the stairs. "My name is Noah."

For several minutes, nothing changed, as though she hadn't heard him. He opened his mouth to try again but stopped when her pale form shuddered and flared like a light bulb flickering before settling back to its initial wattage. She lowered her hands and raised her head, her body rigid as she stopped rocking.

"You can really see me," she whispered.

Noah inched his way closer to the frightened spirit, his hands raised to show he was harmless. "I smiled directly at you that first day we were here. I assumed you could tell."

"No one sees me here. No adult ever has." Her hands shook as she pushed her silver-framed spectacles up the bridge of her nose. "My name is Millie."

"I'm glad to meet you, Millie." He held his hand out to her. She stared at it like it would bite her if she touched it.

"That woman you were with, you called her Claire. Can she see me too?" Millie asked.

Noah chose to read between the lines and answer the question he guessed she really meant. "Don't worry; she didn't hear what you said."

Millie slumped forward and let out a sigh in apparent relief.

He sat down a few feet away from her, crossing his legs in front of him. "She also doesn't know that I can see you or that you're here."

Millie leaned forward, and her gray eyes streaked with gold flashed with interest. She was beautiful. Her lack of modern makeup did nothing to lessen that effect, and she seemed completely unaware of it. Sweeping her chin-length wheat-blonde hair back behind her ears, she licked her lips and pressed them together.

"How is it that you can see me?" Millie asked tentatively.

He shrugged. "I've always been able to. As a kid, my dad

would get angry because I used to talk to 'invisible friends'. Mom understood that I didn't make it up because she saw spirits too. She explained that I couldn't do it in front of other people because they wouldn't understand."

"Do you mind that I'm here?" Millie began to fidget with the hem of her skirt. "You're not going to try to make me leave are you?" She gazed up at him through dark lashes that fluttered like delicate butterflies as she asked.

He didn't want to force her from her home; she had been part of the attraction to buy the property. He loved Claire, but there was something about a conversation with a piece of the past that his fiancée couldn't match. Millie might want to go. If that were the case, he would help her. She may never get this chance again. "Do you want to leave?"

Millie shook her head slowly. "No, and I'm not sure that I could go."

This piqued Noah's curiosity. "What makes you think that?"

She looked away. Her chin trembled with suppressed emotion, and her translucent cheeks brightened in a rosy glow. This little spirit presented a puzzle. Did she blush from shame rather than shyness? Skittish as she was, this was not the time to press her.

"I…" Mille hesitated, took a deep breath and whispered, "I took my own life. I don't think—maybe they won't let me into heaven. I woke up here and never left."

Noah's smile faltered. He reached out a hand to reassure her but stopped short. Surprise didn't cover his feelings. Maybe honor might. It was a privilege that she would divulge something so personal, and he had forgotten himself. Words felt like an inadequate compensation to him for such a confession.

"It's okay," he said at last. "You don't have to talk about it. And I'm not going to make you leave. We'll keep each other company."

chapter 5

illie peered up into Noah's kind blue eyes, which reminded her of a cloudless summer sky with their brightness. They held her gaze, steadying her frazzled nerves. He wanted her company too. Such an idea never occurred to her, but she was glad of it.

"Would you like to watch TV while I unpack the living room boxes? You have seen television right?" Noah asked.

She liked Noah's smile, the way it turned up the corners of his mouth in such an easy way. It was kind like her father's had been.

She nodded. "I've seen it, but it has been a very long time. The previous owner preferred the radio and seldom turned hers on."

"Well then, you've got a lot to catch up on." He stood and walked to the stairs, watching her over his shoulder. "I think I know just what channel to put on for you."

She followed him down, keeping a safe distance. Her lonely heart wanted to trust him, to enjoy the first adult conversation she had participated in since she died, but the part of her that suffered at the hands of her husband, Harold, cautioned her against trust. He too had been charming in the beginning.

Millie clung to her focus on the present, to Noah. As they made their way down to the front room, she pushed aside the fleeting comparison to Harold. Memories lay like traps throughout the house. All it took was one unguarded thought and high-strung emotions to spring it them into action. The last thing she wanted was to find herself sucked inside of one while she was with Noah. Besides one trip into the past was enough for one evening.

They made it without incident to their goal. Stacks of boxes and oversized furniture dominated the room. The centerpiece of this mess was an overstuffed sofa. Noah gestured for her to sit on the monstrosity. She skirted it reluctantly and then sat on the very edge.

He cast a crooked smile in her direction as he dug into a small box. "Get comfortable. It won't swallow you."

Millie scooted back, her hands brushing against the worn leather. She stroked the supple material, soft like a baby's smooth skin. On reflex, she snapped that inner door closed. That way lay heartbreak and danger.

"Got it." He held up a slender black device, triumph in his voice. "Found the remote. Now we're in business."

He pointed it at the large black screen that dominated the wall between the two windows. Leave it to a man to hang the TV first. Of course, the very idea that you could hang a

TV on the wall was a fabulous innovation. How much else had changed in the outside world? She always wondered, and now, Noah was giving her the chance to find out.

"The cable guy was out this afternoon and got us all set up."

Cable, she turned the word over. Certainly wasn't something she had ever heard of, at least not in the way Noah must have meant it. He pointed the handheld device at the black panel on the wall, and it flared to life. Her eyes grew round with wonder as pictures of food and scantily clad people began to fly across the screen, counted off by glowing white numbers in the corner.

"You should see your face right now," Noah laughed. "I thought you'd seen this before?"

Millie nodded absently and leaned towards the images. She had seen TV before, but it hadn't been this vivid or varied—old Mrs. Roosa had only watched four channels. Here there appeared to be dozens. This was a better window to the world outside then she could have hoped for. She could see places she had only ever imagined in books.

The images came to rest on the scene of a house and four people walking towards it. "What is this about?" Millie asked.

She glanced up at Noah. He stood beside the large screen, arms crossed in front of his chest, watching her. His head tilted to the side as though he considered a riddle. "They help people find a new house and then remodel it."

"Oh, like you're doing to my house, right?"

"Yes, exactly." He set the remote down and moved back to the stack of boxes in the corner. "You're okay with that, right? I mean you sounded like you didn't have a problem when you were lecturing my fiancée."

Millie tried to focus on the people taking down cabinets and knocking down walls. He was going to be doing those same things to her childhood home.

"It's a good thing you're doing—truly. It will make it easier for me." She slapped her hand over her mouth.

Noah turned back to her from where he stood unloading books onto the shelf. "Easier? What do you mean?"

A moment's distraction and she was already spilling secrets she had never intended to share, not that she ever had the chance before this. She hugged herself, rubbing her hand up and down her other arm and shrugged.

She stared ahead at the TV, not wanting to make eye contact. "Just that if the house is all fixed up, someone will want to be here. I don't like always being alone."

It was the truth, even if it was only part of it. He stared at her, his blue eyes narrowed in thought. Did he believe her? He let out a distracted "hmm" before returning to his box. He carried it to a table with drawers on the far end of the sofa and sat down on the floor with it.

"What are you doing to the house first?" Millie said as she adjusted her glasses.

Perhaps the distraction would keep him from thinking too hard about what she said before. It would certainly help her to avoid making any more mistakes.

"The bedroom next to the largest bedroom is going to get split into a closet and a new master bathroom," he answered over his shoulder.

"Mother's room already has a closet," she said practically.

"That'll be my closet. The lady of the house requires

something bigger."

Millie scooted across the seat, closer to where Noah was working on unloading slim plastic cases from a box. "Why would she need something bigger? Are you two rich?" She leaned over the arm of the sofa, her arms crossed in front of her. "I wondered that when I saw you the first time. You were both dressed so fine. But if you are, I can't image why you would want my house."

Noah looked up at Millie; his eyes glittered with the smile that stretched across his handsome face. She felt that tingling in her cheeks again and a fluttering feeling that urged her to trust that unguarded look he had. Her mind flashed the image of another smiling face, and Millie frowned. She didn't want to think of that man, not while she was with Noah.

In the pit of her stomach, the uneasy sensation of tilting on an imperceptible axis moved through her. The room slid away around her. She sat properly on her mother's dainty floral sofa. Sunshine that shouldn't be filled the room. She focused on the man sitting in front of her—the real one.

"Millie, are you okay?" Noah's smile faltered. His eyes seemed to search hers.

She focused on his blue eyes, a lifeline to reality. Harold's had been brown.

"I'll be fine," she lied.

"Aren't ya a pretty little thing?" Harold leered at her, his voice quiet, just for her.

"What's going on," Noah said sharply. He started to stand. His brow drew together in a mask of concern. "Did I do something wrong?"

She was supposed to answer Harold, but he wasn't really here. Noah was here. "Tell me why she needs her own closet." Millie struggled to keep her voice even, not show the desperation welling up inside of her.

"Will ya let me talk to ya later?" Harold left his suitcase in the hall and walked towards her. "When yer mama's not around? I'm new in town, and I was hoping we could be friends. Course a girl as sweet as you is probably too busy for the likes of me."

That day, she had been flattered by his attention. At seventeen, no man had ever spoken to her like that. No man had ever noticed her. But she was revolted now and wanted to stay with the man that looked at her with kindness and concern, the man that cared how she felt about the house.

"You aren't seeing me are you?" Noah followed her gaze to the living room entrance. "Who's there, Millie?"

She didn't want to do this. She didn't want to explain it to Noah, to tell him how she suffered. She just wanted him to cover up the bad memories with change so she wouldn't have to fall into them over and over again. If she weren't so worked up about all this change, this wouldn't be happening so soon on the heels of the last memory.

Noah reached out as if to steady her. For a precious second, it stopped. She was on Noah's leather sofa, and she felt him, the impossible weight of his grip on her shoulders anchoring her to the present. How long had it been since someone touched her?

"I been wait'n my whole life to meet a girl like you." Harold said.

Just like that, she lost it. Noah was gone, replaced by the day her life changed irrevocably. God, how she hoped Noah would tear apart this room, so she never had to live this again.

chapter 6

"What channel would you like it on today?" Noah asked her, as he loaded his pockets with his keys and wallet.

"I like that one with all the reality shows. The way people live their lives now, it's so interesting." Millie nestled herself into her favorite corner of the sofa. The monstrous thing was growing on her.

This new routine between them was a minor miracle. She enjoyed the illusion of having a life. Noah had offered to put something on for her nearly every morning in the last few weeks. He had come down for work that first morning and found her on the sofa where she had disappeared the night before. She expected him to push for answers, but he didn't. He just changed the channel and smiled.

Noah chuckled. "I suppose it's quite the culture shock for you."

"Yes, it is. Thank you for allowing me the luxury. I've been learning so much. But I'm sure once your bride moves in this can't continue."

Claire hadn't been in the house once. Millie couldn't understand why she would stay away. Instead, there were nights when Noah left and didn't come home. Millie came to hate those nights. It was as if her memories lay in wait and snatched her away.

Noah shrugged. "I'll work something out. She's coming by tonight to see the progress I've made upstairs. Did you want me to show you how the remote works before I go?"

"No, thank you. I'd rather not damage your TV or drain your remote." Millie chose to address the easiest question first.

She had expected him to ask about the remote before this, but it was as if he used it to distract her from his other statements. Why did he want to divert her from the fact that Claire was coming?

"Thanks, a new one isn't in the budget," he said with a chuckle.

"Don't worry, Noah. I won't do anything to frighten Claire if that's what you're worried about." Why else would he feel the need to announce it to Millie like that—sneaking it in? It was his home too.

Noah's cheeks grew flushed, and he took a step back towards the hall. He looked at the front door and back at her. "You have a nice day."

"Yes, you as well," she said as cheerfully as she could muster. She hoped he would find it reassuring instead of the false note that met her ears.

It seemed to Millie that Noah should be happy rather than nervous that Claire was coming. He bent over backward to please her and make their new home something she could love as much as he so obviously did. Had Millie been blessed to be his wife rather than Harold's, she would have been overcome with gratitude to have such a considerate husband.

Millie sighed wistfully at that little fantasy and settled in to immerse herself in modern living. She focused on the happy couple on the current TV program. Perhaps experience had tempered her view on what Claire should appreciate. Mille regretted the thought as soon as she had it.

The cold came first; it was December in this memory. She relived it enough to know where and when she was, the second the stench of booze struck her. The glow of the low light made Harold look like the very devil, with his sunken eyes cast in shadow. He dragged his hand through greasy hair.

"Gi'me a kiss girl." His words slurred as he grabbed her ankle under the threadbare blanket and dragged her across the bed to him.

Harold leaned over her, adding the smell of sweat to the whisky on his breath. She turned her face away, but he clasped her jaw tight as he pulled her in for that kiss. She felt the bile rise in the back of her throat as his tongue entered her mouth. He released her, pushing her back.

"Where have you been all night, Harold," Millie asked through gritted teeth.

He fell rather than sat on the edge of the bed. The frame shook as if it was about to give under his weight. "Ain't none o' yer business."

"I waited for you all day," She continued. "I needed your pay to go down to the grocers."

"Ain't your money, Millie. I'm the one earn'n it."

She grabbed hold of his shirt collar, forcing him to look her in the eyes. "And I'm your wife. How am I supposed to feed us without the money?"

Harold batted her hand away and stood up. "I didn't ask for no damn wife." He paced the length of their one-room cottage, with its sparse hand-me-down furnishings.

Mille shifted, sitting up on her heels. She clutched the blanket in tight fists. Tears stung her eyes. She hated that she had ever cried for this man. He never deserved those tears.

"I didn't ask for a husband either, but you took me to bed. You made me all sorts of fine promises. This isn't what you promised me, Harold."

The crack across her face came sudden. Even knowing it was coming as she did, she couldn't brace for it. The force of it whipped her around and bounced her head off the wall. She collapsed on the bed and held the side of her face.

"Go home to yer damned mama. Let her feed ya." Harold stalked to the door. The heavy thud of his boots felt like it echoed in her head. "It's my money. I'll drink every penny 'fore I let ya have it."

The door slammed behind him, and Millie was alone, sitting on Noah's deep sofa. She blinked in the bright morning sunlight, not darkness. The pain from that memory still rang in her ears.

chapter 7

"Why did you make the closet so small?"

Balanced on the edge of the oversized tub, Millie watched the power struggle wage between the couple. The gleaming porcelain oval serving as her perch came just this afternoon and dominated the space that once held her bed.

Millie was proud of the work Noah had managed thus far. She expected to hear praise from Claire, or she wouldn't have dared to intrude. But now Millie watched with the fascination one might have for a train wreck. Her conscience told her to respect Noah's privacy, but she couldn't look away.

"You wanted a soaker tub. Where did you think the space was coming from?" Noah threw up his hands from his position leaning against the exterior wall. "It's a second closet. You don't need more than this."

"I thought the space was coming out of your shower." Claire's eyes narrowed as if she was looking for the weak link to pick at and get her way. "How much space do you need?"

When they came up here, Claire had circled the framed out spaces in chilled silence. Her aqua running shoes made no sound as she paraded around in her form-fitting yoga pants, her arms crossed tightly over her chest, stretching the ice blue tank top taut.

Claire scrutinized every inch for the slightest error. How she would know when she came across one, Millie wasn't certain, but she was sure that Claire viewed mistakes only as a tactical advantage to get her own way. Claire looked like a cat, ready to pounce and Noah was her unwitting mouse.

Hope for Claire's good opinion gave way to disappointment as soon as she opened her mouth. If Noah minded that Millie was present for this dressing down, he wasn't showing it—not that he could in front of Claire.

Millie suffered no such constraints. "You're doing all the hard work. I still don't see why she needs a second closet."

Noah's eyes flickered in Millie's direction and then settled back on Claire. She seemed oblivious to the storm brewing, darkening his placid blue eyes to blackened steel.

"I was able to save the baseboards from the new closet." Noah crossed his arms over his chest, mirroring the defensive posture of his fiancée. "I'll reuse them in the master bath. That way everything matches and no waste." Evidently, he had settled on the diplomatic approach of changing the subject to one Millie knew he felt great pride in.

"The waste is to your time. You promised me new finishes."

Millie flinched at Claire's sharp tone. His fiancée glanced up from her flippant inspection of her red-lacquered nails to the scowl developing in Noah's face. Millie lowered herself down from the edge of the tub and drifted back towards the framed-out door until she stood on the other side of the partially finished wall. She continued observing them.

Millie didn't like that look on his face. Having seen it enough on Harold's, it dredged up emotional wounds she would rather not examine. It almost made her miss that on Noah there was an element of control that her deceased husband lacked. Millie was quickly growing to dislike Claire. Despite those feelings, she was nervous for her. Claire had taken her criticism too far.

"Claire just doesn't understand, Noah. She doesn't mean it." Millie found herself feeling the unlikely pull to defend Claire. "You don't have to give in. You're doing right by the house. Just give her a chance to see. Half done, she can't see the vision you have."

Noah kept silent and still as a stone wall. Millie couldn't be sure he listened. Harold would have exploded by now, but Noah hadn't, and that at least gave her some small measure of ease. Claire must also have sensed the miscalculation of her present attitude, or at the very least, that it wouldn't get her what she wanted.

Claire's demeanor shifted from tight and shrewd, to soft and falsely pliant. No longer closing herself off to him, Claire's arms dropped to her sides as she sauntered across the skeletal bathroom to him. She raised one manicured hand to trail down his chest and hook on the waistband of his denim pants.

Her lips puckered into a sultry pout. "You are going to keep your promise, right?"

Noah seemed to squirm in his skin but made no move to

return Claire's attempt at affection. Claire thought they were alone. Millie could see how Claire would think nothing of turning on her womanly charm to get what she wanted. Noah knew better. Again, his eyes darted in Millie's direction.

Claire, refusing to be dissuaded from her goal, reached up and snaked her arms around Noah's neck. She went up on her toes, pulling him into a slow kiss that had Millie seeing red.

A moment ago, Millie had felt sorry for Claire, but this manipulation was disgusting. That wasn't the heart of Millie's feelings, not if she was being honest with herself. If Claire had been kissing anyone else, yes, Millie would have been appalled by her methods, but she would have simply looked the other way. It wasn't her relationship or her place to judge. The fact that Claire was plying her charms on Noah was the issue.

Millie had no right to this swell of jealousy that she was surprised to find burning brightly inside of her. It fueled her, and she felt the energy building like a pressure valve about to blow. His kindness, the hours of conversation and their quiet companionship did not entitle her to anything. Rationally she knew that, but she didn't feel that in this moment.

Claire's hands moved down between them while maintaining the kiss. With a soft moan, she popped the button on his trousers. When she grasped the zipper-pull Noah finally moved, shoving her hand away. Stepping sideways, he broke the kiss and her hold on him.

Millie slumped in relief, but the well of energy her emotions raised did not dissipate. She would have to be careful in this state, or she might find herself inside another memory.

Noah's face was stoic when he opened his mouth to speak. "We need to come to some kind of compromise, but that's not how we're going to get there, Claire."

Claire's face pinched up like a petulant child. Her arms crossed again, this time under her breasts to display the assets he had just turned down and her toe tapped out her impatience.

"I am not giving up the shower for a bigger closet. It costs too much to have the plumber rough it in, and it adds value to the house." Noah paced in front of the gleaming white tub. "I'm also not budging on the baseboards. I'm working hard on them, and it saves us money for the finishes you want."

Claire pounced, her words clipped and her tone harsh. "Fine. Then I want the closet to have custom built-ins. If you're saving so much money on the baseboards, you can afford it."

"Are you kidding me?" Millie practically spat the words as she drifted out from her hiding place to stand in the doorway, hands fisted on her hips. "All of that fuss for a fancier closet? This is ridiculous, Noah. You've done enough."

A bare light bulb hanging down from the corner of the bathroom flickered under the strain of Millie's outburst and then popped, raining down shards of glass. It did nothing to alleviate the pent-up well of energy.

Claire shrieked as she did a little jump step to the side. "What the hell!"

Noah closed his eyes and reached up to pinch the bridge of his nose.

As if to steady himself, he took a series of deep breaths in through the nose and out through the mouth. "Fine, I will look into a customizable closet system for you. Satisfied?"

A moment of strained silence passed between them. Claire shifted and then finally broke the stalemate. "For now."

Her words were a challenge, whether or not Noah saw it—

Millie did. She wanted to scream out her frustration. This woman was getting a beautiful home that she didn't have to work for. She just had to show up. Yet not only did she make demands, she expected him to sacrifice the things he liked about it and showed not an ounce of appreciation.

Restless and brooding, Millie paced behind Noah, wishing there was some way she could shove Claire into a wayward memory. It could do Claire good to learn the humility Millie had to at Harold's hands. She shook herself, regretting that she had such a hateful notion. No one deserved to live the tormented life that she had that last year.

Millie fled the room and the manipulation she had just witnessed. She wanted to forget this whole episode had happened and return to the vibrant world in the television. She made it only as far as the bottom of the stairs before her will gave out and she collapsed.

Energy still rolled within Millie, simmering on a slow boil, but it would not carry her non-corporeal form any further. Venting it at something, or more appropriately someone, held a strong appeal. She couldn't have imagined that she would regret the promise she had freely offered. There would be no frightening Claire. The light bulb had not been intentional, and she was not about to allow jealousy to break her moral fortitude, no matter how sorely tempted she might be.

The storming couple moved in Millie's direction. Mired in her own thoughts, she chose to ignore the voices and their proximity. It wasn't worth the effort to move out of their path despite the uncomfortable pressure she felt when she allowed Claire to walk right through her.

Millie pressed her hands to her chest as if the experience

had left a gaping hole to fill.

Claire shivered and stumbled. She would have fallen down the last step had Noah not sidestepped Millie and caught Claire's elbow.

Noah gave Millie a sharp look and turned back to Claire. "Are you alright?"

"I'm fine." Claire jerked her elbow from his grasp. "I'm going home, alone."

Her gaze bounced from wall to wall in the entryway. Millie knew she was looking for an air vent. Some easy explanation for the cold spot she passed through.

"I think you need to have the AC system checked or something." Claire pulled the front door open. "I told you this place was a money pit."

The door closed with a heavy thud. Noah leaned his forehead into it and spoke without looking at Millie. "I thought you said you were going to leave her alone."

"I did." Her answer was quiet, barely above a whisper. "I just sat here."

If he only understood how she felt, how much she had wanted to do. He might have applauded her restraint at only sitting on the stairs. But then he couldn't know that she was still reeling in the throes of jealousy, something she knew she had no right to feel. It was a surprise even to herself.

"And she doesn't know you're there. You could have moved." Noah sighed heavily, as though he couldn't muster the energy to be angry with her. "It's late, and I'm not going to get any work done. What do you say you and I settle in for the night with some home improvement shows?"

Noah watched her, his face pinched into a sad and defeated

expression. If that was how Claire made him feel, Millie had to wonder why he would do so much for her, why he would marry her. Millie wanted nothing more than to bring back his smile. All she had to offer was companionship, and if that would be enough, she would not withhold it.

"I think an evening with you sounds lovely." After all, soon his bride would stand between them, as surely as she had over a closet.

chapter 8

oah pushed the faded orange cart slowly through the tile department of the home improvement store, taking slow, deep breathes to remain calm. "Claire, I really need you to pick something in stock. We don't have time to special order anything. The tile has to be laid this week if you want the master suite done before our wedding."

"But I want something special, not cookie cutter. I don't want *stock* finishes. That's why you talked me into a fixer-upper, remember?" Claire complained.

Noah smiled weakly at an elderly couple giving them a sideways glance as they ambled past. They probably took one look at his blue jeans and well-loved Thor t-shirt and thought Claire was slumming it. Too bad, they didn't know about his MBA. He wasn't making six-figures yet, but he was further up the corporate ladder then she pretended to be.

Claire looked out of place in this hardhat haven, wearing

her designer label silk blouse and the pencil skirt that hugged her curves enough to remind him that he should consider himself a lucky man. Instead, the pale blue and charcoal grey that she thought made her look classy made him think of ice, which is what the blood in his veins felt like near her over the last several weeks.

Each click of Claire's red-soled heels echoed like the seconds ticking down on the time bomb of their wedding. He promised her he would get it done, but she wanted an upgrade to everything and took forever to make the smallest choice. So much so that on anything he thought he could get away with, he stopped asking her so that he could make up for lost time. He was not about to hear another *I told you so* from her.

Pinching the bridge of his nose, he closed his eyes before he spoke. "Picking in-stock tile does not mean we have *stock* finishes. It's the combination we put together that makes it special."

"I don't know why you're getting so pissy with me. It's not easy planning a wedding and our new home," she grumbled as she dug through her purse. "It's a lot of pressure to do everything perfect. You just have to show up at our wedding and install what I pick out at the house."

"Yeah, so easy after an eight hour day at the office," he shot back. "If I'm not working or sleeping, I'm building at the house."

"The house that you wanted. You wanted to do this. I wanted move-in ready." Unearthing her inhaler, Claire shook it before bringing it to her red painted lips and drawing deeply from it.

Noah turned and walked away, to the end of the aisle. It

had been like this almost as soon as they had gotten engaged, meaningless argument after meaningless argument. Usually, he gave in, gave her whatever made her happy. It had to be the wedding planning that was stressing her out. At least he hoped so because he was beginning to feel as though he made the biggest mistake of his life.

The first disagreement he had come out ahead on in quite some time was the house. But then that had effected their overall future and not just the wedding. Claire never seemed happy with anything he did; she always pushed for more. At this point, going home to Millie looked more and more appealing. Every night he literally tore her house—the place she was born and died in—down to the studs and turned it into something new. Millie never complained. In fact, she told him she was grateful that someone loved her house enough to do it.

A compliment had yet to pass through Claire's tarted up lips.

Resigned to get through this, he walked back to his fiancée, stopping first to grab a 12x12 sheet of tile and a handful of white subway tile. "What do you think of this? We can do the white penny tile on the floor, and I can lay the subway tile in the shower in a herringbone pattern? With your black vanity and white vessel sink, it'll look classic but with a modern twist."

His description sounded like the something a designer would say on one of those shows he watched with Millie. But if it sold the concept to Claire and they could get out of this store, he didn't care.

"I haven't seen that in any of the houses we toured before, and I do like how it sparkled. You have my attention." Claire crossed her arms in front of her and cocked her head at an angle, her lips pursed in consideration.

"We have your soaker tub going in, I'd go with the polished chrome faucets, and we can paint the walls that revere pewter color that you said you like."

"Oiled bronze is easier to clean," she commented.

As if she didn't hire in for that, but he kept that thought to himself. "Then we'll go with that."

chapter 9

Something weighed on Noah's mind—Millie could see it plainly. When he came home with the tile and vanity, something had changed. It wasn't that he treated her any different. It was the way they were together that was different; he was quieter, more absorbed in his own thoughts. This wasn't the first night she noticed the alteration. After the blowup over the closet, Millie observed a pattern. When he spent any amount of time with Claire, he was not as full of the easy conversation Millie had grown to crave.

Usually, it wore off after a few hours of work on the bathroom that created the original source of tension. Millie observed him as he worked, laying square sheets of dainty round tile. When her husband had brooded like this, he had taken to drinking. So far, she hadn't spotted any sign of it on Noah. Just the silence.

Silence she could handle, but from Noah, it unnerved her.

"I like the pattern on the walls of the shower." Millie stroked the glossy white porcelain. Her voice was steady, concealing the anxiety pulsating in her chest where her heart now lay still. "The lady on TV called that herringbone. Is that right?"

Noah sat back on his heels to admire his progress. Reaching up, he dragged his forearm across his brow to mop up the sweat dripping into his thick eyelashes. Millie admired the view of his blue t-shirt stretched across strong shoulders, almost as much as she liked the previous image of his worn denim from behind.

He raised an eyebrow at her. "Are you sure you're admiring my tile work?"

The amused twinkle in his eye filled Millie with relief, and she giggled at the new buoyant sensation that replaced the fluttering nerves. "I may be dead, but I'm certainly not blind."

Noah eased back against the wall and stretched out his legs. "Now seems like a good time for a break."

"Yes, you've been working so hard. I worry about you."

Millie hesitated, weighing her words. She could let things go as they were, but she genuinely cared for Noah. If her unexpected jealousy was any indication, her feelings ran deeper than she dared admit. There were needs she could never fill for Noah—no matter what her heart may want—but sounding board was one she could satisfy.

Fixing her eyes on the stubble that lined his jaw, she pressed on. "You seem as though something is bothering you lately. If you don't mind my saying, it seems worse when you've been with Claire."

Noah sighed heavily. "Does anything get past you?"

"Not when you've spent decades observing people as your sole means of entertainment." Giving up on avoiding eye contact, Millie moved to sit directly across from Noah so that she could look straight into the stormy blue depths of his eyes.

"Things have been strained lately. She was always a little demanding before the engagement. It just seems to have gotten so much worse. And since I talked her into this house..."

"I've noticed she is quick to remind you whose idea this was."

"Every time we're in the same room," he lamented.

Noah's head fell back against the wall, and he stared up at the ceiling.

"You've worked so hard to please her." Millie's voice came out small. "I would have been grateful if Harold had done anything for me, let alone what you've done to give her everything she asks for."

Noah sighed and scrubbed his hand down his face as if to brush off the frustration, as he had wiped away the sweat of his brow.

"Claire didn't choose any of this." His arm swept out, gesturing to the tile that surrounded them. "She demanded high-end, custom everything. More than I could afford, so she dug her heels in. In the end, I made suggestions, and she just agreed to it. Of course, when it's done, she'll tell everyone she knows that I was just the muscle."

Millie traced the penny-sized white tiles on the floor with one finger. "It's beautiful, Noah. I look forward to seeing it finished. My mother would have loved it."

He smiled at her, and pleasure radiated through her like sunshine that her admiration made him happy.

"Do you mind if I ask you something, Millie?"

She nodded her acceptance, and he pressed on. "Since I met you, you've rarely mentioned your family. Tonight you've mentioned both your mother and this Harold. I haven't wanted to pry but…Who was Harold?"

She expected the question to sting or worse pull her into another memory. For once, she felt nothing but emptiness and her surroundings remained unchanged. She opened her mouth once to answer and closed it.

When she tried again, her voice came out a hushed whisper. "My husband."

Noah's eyes widened, and his eyebrows shot up in shock before he was able to school his expression into something more even-keeled. "You look too young."

"I took my life just after I turned eighteen," she said matter-of-factly.

He leaned forward, his gaze penetrating and pinched with concern as he braced his forearms on his drawn up knees. "You strike me as such a happy person. I have trouble reconciling the woman I see before me, and the girl who took her own life. Why?"

Noah's expression was so full of compassion. This was not an idle curiosity; he really saw her and that more than anything made her want to share her secrets.

"For you to understand, I'd have to tell you the whole long story." Millie pulled off her spectacles to swipe at the spectral tears that were already building as she turned inward.

She looked down at the silver frames clasped in her hands, not brooding, but contemplative. After so many years of forced reflection, she had attained the distance to see most of her life for what it had been.

"You have my undivided attention."

"At the end of the Depression, my parents took boarders when they could, to help make ends meet." Millie drew her knees up to her chest, careful to tuck her skirt around her. "My father worked but times were hard, and we were a large family. Harold worked with my father, and he came to stay with us. Harold was the first man who had ever noticed me."

Millie took a deep breath, dreading the next part, or rather the telling of it.

Anxious to get it be rid of the burden, the words tumbled out in a mad rush. "I got pregnant, and we eloped on Halloween."

She looked up at Noah, expecting to see judgement in his eyes, but found none. While she had been speaking, he had moved closer, almost touching her faded spectral form. His head tilted to one side in what appeared to be consideration, without any of the censure she had expected to find.

His apparent acceptance gave her the courage she needed to continue. "My parents were angry, but they still loved me, so my father and Harold built a small one-room cottage at the back of this property. I believe you use it as the garage now."

"You lived in that tiny one stall garage!"

Millie almost laughed at Noah's outrage over her meager living accommodations, especially considering he showed no reaction to her unplanned pregnancy and elopement. For the time she had been lucky to have the cottage, and in church, she had often heard condescending busybodies whisper that it was more than she deserved considering the choices she made.

"I was happy to have it," Millie said. "And things were

fine at first, but as I grew large with the baby, Harold became distant and drank away his pay every night. If I ate at all, it was scraps my mother had saved. She did her best to keep me healthy for the baby, but she didn't know how bad it had gotten and my own foolish pride kept me from telling her."

"Did he ever hit you, Millie?" Quiet anger filled Noah's voice.

Before she could read into his tone and the source of the emotion behind it, her mind flashed to that bitter night in December. She raised her fingers to trail over the side of her face as though she could still feel the echo of Harold's hand and the dull ache where her head connected with the wall.

"Only once," she whispered. "I learned to avoid it after that. Harold's sin was neglect, and his weapon of choice was words."

The knuckles of Noah's clenched fists stood out, bone white. Millie wasn't sure how to feel about this show of emotion from him. She imagined that it was akin to the anger and jealousy she felt towards Claire, but for him, there could be no outlet, no one to berate since the object of that rage was long past dead. If this much of her story made Noah angry, the rest wouldn't fare much better.

"Mother and I were pregnant at the same time. She gave birth before me. My son came in April, at least a month before he should have. He was so small, but then I was half starved." Millie's voice broke. She looked away, tears of shame stinging her eyes. "My mother nursed him for me…I wasn't able. We kept him warm in a basket on the over door. None of it made a difference. He died the week after he was born."

"I'm so sorry," Noah offered simply, his tone a somber whisper.

Millie couldn't look at him, not if she wanted to finish this. She pressed on, anxious just to finish dredging that part of her life. "Harold became so much worse after that, screaming at me about my failure as a woman and a mother. I don't know how much of it my father got wind of, but one night Harold didn't come home, My older brother told me that he and father took care of him down at the pool hall and I'd have an annulment. I should have been happy, but I was damaged goods, a girl with loose morals, and mourning the loss of my son. It became too much to bear."

Her tale of woe unburdened for the first time since her passing, the black mass that sat in the void below where her heart had been, lifted and allowed her tears to flow freely. The glistening moisture rolled down her transparent cheeks to disappear harmlessly. She shook with the effort not to sob. There had been no one else to tell. Had she been able to, she still wasn't sure that she would have been up to it before this— before him.

Noah reached out with his hand to brush the tear from her face, as though he had forgotten in the moment that the girl in front of him was intangible. His hand passed harmlessly through her, and he snatched it back, cradling it to his chest in surprise.

"Oh, Millie." Maybe it was her own desires playing games with her, but those simple words held a note of longing along with the more appropriate feelings rolling between them.

"Don't fret over me," Millie stood to gain distance. "The world has moved on since then, and you should too."

Millie smiled weakly as him as she backed towards the

door, ready to retreat to the sanctuary of the attic. Noah's hands rested flat on the floor, bracing his weight, where he had fallen forward in his attempt to comfort her. The tears welling in his eyes brimmed over the edge like a swollen river.

Unable to stand the reflection of her own sorrow and his empathy, she caved to the base instinct to flee. He called her name, but she couldn't stop until her back rested against the other side of the closed attic door. When the seconds ticked by in silence, a tiny piece of her heart, no doubt the same one that had urged her to tell him her story, was disappointed he didn't follow her. She reached up and rested her hand over the imprints her tears left behind on her face.

She savored the tingling that remained from his attempt to touch her.

chapter 10

i don't know how you manage in this kitchen," complained Claire as she pulled two plates down from the cabinet over the dishwasher, a convenience the space didn't have the month before. "There's hardly any storage, and we're going to have more stuff then we'll know what to do with from all our wedding presents."

Noah unpacked the cashew chicken and steamed rice, handing it off to Claire, as he watched Millie through the open doorway descending the last few stairs. Seeing her, his thoughts drifted to the tingling in his fingers the other night, when he'd felt compelled by her shimmering trail of tears to touch her face.

Losing a child and being run down by a man who obviously didn't deserve her was too much for any young woman, let alone the tenderhearted and animated woman he had come to cherish. Depression and life's cruelty may have driven her to a premature death, but it hadn't tempered her sweetness.

"Are you listening to me," Claire asked, breaking his reverie.

Noah did a once over of the woman he was supposed to be marrying, hoping for a feeling other than irritation to surface. Her querulous tone and the frustrated rhythm of her lacquered nails tapping on the new butcher-block counters grated his nerves, but that was all. He couldn't even muster attraction for her in the short jean skirt and red halter-top as she stood leaning one hip against the cabinets.

She was dressed for going out and had been pissed to find him in stained work jeans and a t-shirt with the sleeves torn off, still tiling upstairs.

A month ago, the curves that her ensemble put on tempting display would have done him in. The graceful curve of her neck, bare thanks to her upswept hair, and those pouty lips that she kept slick with red gloss would have had him panting like a dog at her feet. How had things ever gotten this far with her?

Claire's face scrunched up at his continued silence and his casual perusal of her. She sighed and cocked her head to one side, brows raised in question.

Noah shrugged, "I don't think it will really be a problem. Any duplicates from our single lives will get donated to make way for the new."

Rolling her eyes, Claire grabbed her plate and moved to the table ahead of Noah.

He'd found the farmhouse table on Craigslist, sanded it down, and stained the top a rich walnut before painting the base and ladder back chairs "mint sorbet". Millie picked the pastel paint color, proclaiming it something that her mother would have loved to have in her kitchen. It added a nice feminine touch to the room's freshly painted white cabinets.

Claire's reaction had been just another "why isn't this custom" argument, a direction he felt this conversation being pulled in now. Lately, it felt as if her visits were just to find fault.

"I hope you plan on redoing this kitchen next year. I need a gourmet kitchen," Claire pointed around the room with a fork full of food. "This isn't it. Frankly, I'm not sure why you wasted your time on this instead of ripping it out now. Besides, where did you get the idea that I'd even like white cabinets?"

"It's so beautiful this way. I think you did a lovely job, Noah. She should appreciate your effort more," Millie commented from the kitchen doorway.

Noah struggled to keep from smiling at Millie's appreciation. He doubted that Claire would take it well.

"I had to pinch and scrape the budget to do what I did. I figured a small update was better than white and gold Formica and avocado appliances." Noah shoved a fork full of chicken into his mouth.

"You *figured* wrong," Claire said. "I'd rather you spent the money on the bigger closet I wanted upstairs or some other upgrade."

Noah took his time chewing, using it to keep his calm.

He swallowed and waited a beat before he continued, his voice even and tone dry. "Maybe if you didn't borrow money from the house budget to put towards the wedding, I could have done those things or made the kitchen better."

"She *stole* from you?" Millie exclaimed as she drifted behind Claire's shoulder. "How can you marry someone who would do that?”

Claire slammed down her fork in a fit of indignation. “Our wedding is important! Don’t you want it to be special?”

“It’s just one day. What’s important is the commitment we’re making and our future together, which will be lived in this house.”

“Um, no,” Claire said, sitting back and crossing her arms in front of her. “This is a starter home. In five years, we’ll flip it and move on to a bigger better one.”

Millie paced behind Claire, clearly unsettled. “You can’t leave. Tell her you’re staying. I don’t want to go back to a big empty house with no one to talk to.” Millie stopped and focused on him. “*You* can’t leave me.”

“What gave you that idea? I never agreed to flip it and move on,” Noah replied, an answer for Millie as much as it was a rebuttal to Claire.

“Why else would I agree to move into a rundown farm house,” Claire shouted.

“Because of the opportunity. A diamond in the rough that needed some love and a family to bring it back to life. That could be us, Claire.” Noah reached across the table for her hand, but she pulled away and stood up.

“I don’t need your permission. I tried to make you happy, Claire. Really, I did, but what you seem to forget is that my name and my money bought this house and paid for this renovation. You need to decide if you want a place in this dream.”

“Maybe I don’t. So, where does that leave us, Noah?”

Millie drifted up beside Claire once more, hands held over her heart, as if whatever his answer, it held something meaningful for her.

"I don't know, Claire. I think that's really up to you," he answered softly.

"Suddenly, I'm not so sure I want to get married next week."

Claire grabbed her purse off the kitchen counter and marched away. Stopping at the back door, she looked back at him, expectantly. When it registered that he had to intention of stopping her, her lips pressed thin into a tight frown, before her expression hardened and she strode briskly out the door.

Noah waited to feel disappointment, but he just didn't. Instead, he watched Millie as she came around the table towards him. Concern over his fiancée should have been at the forefront of his mind. In its place, he worried over this vibrant spirit of a woman, intangible to the rest of the world, but seen and cared for by his heart.

Millie hadn't changed in the weeks since he'd met her, just as Claire hadn't. The ghostly woman he shared so much with had the same blonde bob and wire-rim glasses. The same ill-fitting white dress hung on her thin frame. Her exterior was simple, but she was never plain. Her grey eyes with their flecks of hazel gold reminded him of the sun peeking through a storm cloud, and the soft blush of her cheek was her natural beauty, nothing artificial or painted on.

Noah was the one who had changed, or rather his perception had. The fog that had obscured his path had burned away under the warmth of Millie's radiance.

"You're not getting married—you're done with her." She said it like a statement, rather than questioning her as he had expected.

"I've been done. I just didn't know it until now. Every

change I made in this house, I did it for you." He hadn't admitted it before now, but it was true.

When he suggested the tile upstairs, in the back of his mind, he was aware that his suggestions would make Millie happy. He had outright allowed Millie to choose the finish for the kitchen, all the while lying to himself that it was for Claire. The house, and the woman trapped in it had drawn him from the first.

"You brought my home back to life," Millie said her tone soft. "I wish it could be the same for me. I can't even touch you. You deserve so much more."

Her tongue darted out to moisten her full lips before she nervously clamped her bottom lip between her teeth.

Noah reached out his hand to touch her, but remembering the other night, he stopped without making contact. "I deserve you."

"You want to live with me and never touch." Unshed tears balanced precariously in her eyes, making the gold streaks sparkle like the sun on water. "You'd never have children, a family. No one would understand."

"You'd rather that I marry her and have those things?"

Millie shook her head. The movement allowed the tears to escape and roll down her china white face. "Not her, but someone better than her."

He stepped in closer, just a breath separating them. Her neck craned back to look up into his eyes. Unable to touch her, the distance might as well have been miles.

"What if there's no one better than you?" Noah asked.

Millie's form faded in and out like a flickering candle. It reminded him of the moments when she disappeared, and for a heartbeat, he worried she would leave him. Something about this seemed different. He felt her presence with him, but the possibilities hovered dangerously near, and with so much unresolved between them his nerves refused to settle.

"I'm here," she whispered, answering his unexpressed concern.

She faded to a mere wisp of fog. If he waved his hand through her body, surely she would dissipate. To his shock, he felt her—her little fingers pressing gently on the back of his neck, pulling him in.

Tender and unsure, she kissed him.

He responded slowly, stunned this moment could happen. Knowing he might never have this chance again, he poured himself—his love—into this one kiss, this magic moment. He reached up to cradle her face in his hands. As he touched her, whatever had blessed this moment broke apart and with it his heart.

His lips, hands, and neck tingled with the memory of her touch.

"I'm so sorry, Noah. I wasn't strong enough to give you more." Millie's voice held the longing that echoed in him.

Shaking and faded, she collapsed to the floor at his feet.

Noah knelt in front of her, aching with the need to touch her again and comfort her. "It happened once, it can happen again. Please don't give up."

Spectral tears flowed freely now as Millie rose slowly. Every small movement seemed to drain her further. Noah reached out his hand to help her, and it passed through her. Her eyes filled with pain as she stepped back until his hand no longer protruded from her shoulder.

Millie staggered away from him in silence. When she reached the door, she stumbled. Reaching out to brace herself, her hand passed through the wall—something he had never seen her do. By force of will alone, she managed to stay erect and drag herself from the room.

chapter 11

millie sat by her rosette window, leaning against the exposed wood lath, absorbing the warmth of the sun. She held her hand up, the golden stream of light passing through her transparent fingers. To her own eyes, she solidified in the restorative warmth, but it didn't bring the peace and contentment it normally washed her in. Instead, she chafed at her own weakness.

A soft tap sounded on the attic door. "Millie?"

Her lashes fluttered shut against the tears that rushed forward. The door remained closed. With silent footfalls, she moved down the attic stairs, stopping on her side of the door.

"I just want to know that you're all right." Noah's voice trembled.

Millie laid her hand against the door. Was he doing the same on the other side? It was his warmth she wanted, not the suns. She reached for the door handle but pulled her hand back and rested her forehead against the painted wood.

She couldn't face him yet, weak as a kitten. Not until she decided what to do.

Say something, she pleaded silently. A tear slipped free and rolled a lazy trail down her cheek. The moisture disappeared into nothingness before it hit the floor.

Millie heard Noah whisper. "I love you. Please be okay."

His heavy footsteps retreated down the hall, followed by the rhythmic pounding of his descent down the stairs. She sank to the floor to gather her scattered emotions.

Noah loved her or thought he did. It was what she wanted, but it wasn't right. She told him the truth last night, even though the words burned in her throat. She could never give him the life he deserved.

Millie shook herself and scurried up the attic steps, back to the window in time to see Noah's car back down the driveway. No longer concerned about a chance encounter, she went down to the living room.

He left the TV on her favorite channel.

Millie sighed to herself. He was always so thoughtful, but tearful brides shopping for the perfect dress did not help her melancholy mood. She settled into the plush embrace of the sofa to watch it at first, crying over the parade of happy brides. She had never been a happy bride.

The first tug of silken threads dragged at her. She brushed at her face, to push them away as if that was possible. The web of her emotions snared her tighter with the feeble struggle, dragging her into the memory.

The tink, tink, tink of pebbles striking glass cut through her senses and when she blinked, she was not in front of the

TV. She sat hugging her knees in the darkness on her childhood bed. The moon cut a swath of light across her floor and the pink rose pattern on her quilt. It gleamed off the brass bedpost. If she had it to do again, she wouldn't have gone to that window. Not this night or any other that Harold came. Here she was just an automaton without choice, reliving the memory.

Millie slipped off the edge of the bed. Rushing to the window before he woke her parents, she lifted it and leaned out the casement. "Harold, what are you doing?"

He stood crushing his hat in his hands, looking up at her with the crooked smile that made her heart skip the first time he had turned it her way. "Come on down, Millie. Don't be like that."

"I'm coming," she said with a girlish giggle that offended her own ears.

Millie pulled her head back in and swung her first leg out so that she straddled the window and then pulled the other out. Harold put his cap on and reached up to her. With a silent prayer, she leaped down into his arms. It was a big leap, but he was a tall man, and this was not the first time he caught her. He stumbled back but held firm before swinging her down for her feet to touch the ground.

Harold took her hand, and they ran to her father's barn. Her heart raced with fear for the future that lay ahead. As soon as they were out of sight behind the barn doors, Harold swung her into his arms, lifting her up to kiss him. Her feet dangled like a child.

In the moment, she was simultaneously nervous and excited. Reliving it, her gut rolled in disgust over the tobacco taste of his mouth and the overwhelming stench of animals and hay around them. She might be forced into the reenactment and the emotions that came with it, but she did not have to enjoy it.

"Sweet girl, I've been wait'n for this all day." It was the last romantic or even nice thing he ever said to her.

He backed her up against the barn wall and reached for the edge of her skirt. His rough hand slid up her thigh. Relaxing into him, her body arched forward, but her mind wanted his hands off her. In retrospect, she knew it had only ever been lust for him, and she was just the silly young girl that fell for it.

"Harold, slow down." Millie struggled to catch her breath as he buried his face in her neck, his stubble scraping against her skin. "I have something to tell you."

He stopped, waiting for her to speak as his body ground into her, a reminder of what he wanted, pinning her against the wall. She struggled to think past the wave of desire muddling her already chaotic thoughts.

Her words came out in a rush. "I'm pregnant."

Millie landed on her rear; the shock of it sent an ache up her spine.

He paced back and forth in front of her. "Dammit, Millie. How could this happen?"

From the floor, she stared up at him, her eyes wide. "What are we going to do?"

"You haven't told your mama and daddy, have ya?" He asked, still moving.

"Goodness no. I wanted to tell you first." She felt heat rising in her face. Anxiety coursed through her. Knowing what was coming, she was powerless to stop the words flowing out of her mouth. "But it's going to be okay right? You said we'd always be together."

"I know what I said," Harold snapped as he stopped in front of her.

Looking at that scowl, she wished she had never said the words—wished he had never entered her father's house. He pulled out a flask she had not seen before that night and took a swig. He dragged his sleeve over his mouth and returned the foul thing to his jacket pocket.

"Come on then," his voice was gruff, almost a growl.

He snatched at her hand, dragged her off the floor and out the barn door, muttering to himself as he carted her behind him. "Was this yer plan, trap'n me like this?"

"No, Harold. You said…" The tears started rolling, but she choked back a sob that threatened to break free. "Where are we going?"

Millie stumbled, and Harold glared back over his shoulder at her. His expression was black as he yanked her upright without a break in his stride.

"Where do ya think? Get'n hitched, so yer daddy don't string me up."

chapter 12

illie shook herself from the past.

Now she truly loved someone, and not just someone but a man who treated her with kindness, who cared about her wellbeing, who valued her as she was.

Now someone loved her back and was willing to give up the future he had planned to find a way to be with her. What could she give him for such devotion? She didn't even have the strength to touch him. She would never be able to deliver him the son he deserved. She had done that for a husband who neglected her cruelly, leaving her and their unborn son to starve. She blamed herself for not being strong enough to make her baby healthy, but now she understood where the blame truly fell.

Now she laid the fault soundly on the feet of the man who drank away the money that should have nourished them.

She couldn't watch this show anymore. She needed to think, not wallow in self-pity. Having no way to turn the TV off, she left the room, drifting towards the kitchen. It was plain to see that Noah had not bothered to come back in here last night. Chairs sat abandoned, pushed back from the table, plates, and silverware with the food now cold and forgotten.

Millie couldn't leave her home or Noah, but she couldn't stay and watch him love someone else. Prior to last night, Millie at the least reconciled herself to his marriage plans, but now—he loved her back, and that changed everything.

"If you love someone let them go," she told herself.

Her mother, God rest her soul, had told her that when Harold hadn't come home. Millie never really loved Harold, not the way she loved Noah; she had clung to her husband in naiveté and desperation.

She would have to convince Noah to marry Claire, or if not her, someone else. If he wouldn't listen, she would hide from him. Maybe if he didn't see her, he would move on. Millie leaned against the counter and sighed heavily. Yeah, like he would really listen to her or let her hide. More importantly, she wasn't so sure she could stay away.

The back door opened and the screen door clanged shut, shattering the silence and Millie's tenuous hold on peace. She looked up, expecting to find Noah staring back at her, but found Claire instead.

Claire set down her grocery bags and leaned against the counter, unknowingly mirroring Millie. Her phone clutched in one hand, she kicked off her shoes. As her icy blue eyes scanned her surroundings, she coughed into the back of her hand.

"No, I can't let him cancel the wedding," Claire said to the person on the other end of the conversation. Her voice raspy with the effort to speak. "I'm going to make him dinner and turn on the charm. I don't have another choice."

Claire cleared the dishes from the table and scraped the plates into the garbage with the phone pinched between her shoulder and her cocked head.

Millie eyed her tight jeans, low cut top, and pouty red lips. She had certainly dressed to do the job, but Claire did not look well. Her breathing came out heavy and labored; there were bags under her eyes, and her face had a sickly pale sheen.

"I don't need my inhaler, I'm just upset," Claire said, as if in answer to Millie's thoughts. "I can't stand up in front of all those people and tell them to take back the gifts, there won't be a wedding. I just can't do it."

Millie rolled her eyes; she hopped up to sit on the counter and watch, with her ankles crossed primly. It didn't surprise her that shame motivated Claire, rather than love.

"No, I'm not telling him about the baby."

Millie snapped to attention at this new information.

Claire continued, "I'll tell him on our honeymoon like I planned to."

A coughing fit racked Claire's body for several long minutes. She covered the mouthpiece of her phone, hiding the sound, as she listened to the person on the other end of the line.

"Because he wouldn't believe me right now. I do not want him to feel obligated to marry me. That's only a last resort," Claire shouted at the phone before dropping it.

Claire grabbed the counter with one hand, struggling to

stay upright. She snatched her purse and dragged it to the floor as she went down. Claire frantically dumped the contents onto the floor, clutching at her throat with her other hand.

Millie jumped down off the counter and backed her way along the wall, frightened by Claire's struggle for air. Millie flashed back to her own struggle to breathe as the noose tightened and she swung from the attic rafters. The tips of her toes grazed the stool beneath her.

When the memory cleared, she found herself kneeling before Claire's prone body. The French manicured nails that had ceased to scratch her delicate throat turned blue, her eyes rolled back, and she lay still as the color drained from her face.

"I can't stand in front of all those people and tell them," said Claire's spirit as she sat across from Millie, looking over the top of her body. "Maybe it's better this way."

"What about the baby?" Millie's arms folded protectively over her own stomach, remembering what she went through to have her child and the pain of losing him.

"Noah doesn't need to know," Claire answered. "Have you come to take me to heaven?"

"No, I'm Millie. I live in the house."

Claire's face scrunched up in confusion for a moment, but it passed quickly. "You could tell them for me? Tell them the wedding is off and that I'm sorry?"

Millie sat back on her heels, her mind reeling with the possibility Claire had offered. A second chance at life, with Noah and a child—to experience real love.

She grappled with the moral implications. Was it right to take advantage, when she should be talking the dying woman into going back? But if Claire freely made the choice who was she to deny her?

The room suddenly became blindingly bright. As it dimmed, both women looked up at the light, glowing warmly from the kitchen doorway. Heaven—had it finally come to collect her? *I don't want to leave.*

Claire smiled back at Millie as she stood to go. "Thank you for telling them."

Claire walked into the light.

That was it—"them"—appearances. No thought for Noah, the man she was to marry, the father of the child in her dying body or even for the child. No care for what they deserved—just like Harold hadn't cared.

Millie had seconds to decide before the light would be gone and this chance passed. Her heart knew what it wanted, what everyone deserved, no matter whether it was right or wrong.

Millie laid down in Claire's body, and her long dulled perception became flooded with sensations, as this new body fought to hold on. Her chest and throat burned. If there had been anyone to hear her cry for help, she couldn't have. As her vision began to fade to black, a familiar clang echoed through the kitchen and her heart.

"Claire! Why are you—oh my God, hang on," Noah yelled.

Millie could hear banging, then the press of his hand in hers and the warmth of his body beside hers. A body, she could physically feel him and would experience more if she could just make it a little longer.

"I've got your inhaler," Noah's clipped words projected tension and fear. "Can you sit up?"

When she couldn't respond, Noah reached under her back, lifting her just enough to tilt her head, while he shook the inhaler. The plastic tube pressed to her mouth and a puff of medication released down her throat.

Seconds passed, and the pressure eased, but not enough. Millie could hear him dialing the phone and talking to someone. Then the plastic tube pressed to her mouth again, and the heaviness in her chest and throat improved more. She drew in a shallow breath that made a horrible wheezing sound. Then the coughing started. Noah helped her lean forward, the weight on her chest lifted, and she was able to cough more.

"You've never had an attack this bad before. How did this happen?" he asked.

"I was upset," she rasped out.

She looked him in the eyes, silently willing him to understand. Grabbing his hand, she pressed it to her stomach.

"Baby—I had to tell you…" Another spasm of coughing rocked Millie's new body, stealing her words.

"Shit, Claire—it's going to be okay. I called an ambulance."

Millie was sick of hearing that name. Though she felt gratitude for this second chance, she didn't want to lie. She opened her mouth to correct Noah, but more coughing replaced her words.

As they waited, she couldn't seem to stop the wave of coughing fits. More than anything, she wanted to marry Noah and carry his baby. Noah pulled her onto his lap, his steady presence anchoring her and sealing her decision. When the convulsion finally ended, the EMTs were there and took her away.

chapter 13

Strapped down on a stretcher was not how Millie imagined leaving the house for the first time in decades. Add to that the harrowing ambulance ride, nurses and EMTs with questions she couldn't answer, the cloying stench of antiseptic, and needles—it went on and on. Making it to the relative calm of an exam room with Noah still at her side had been a boon.

Vanilla walls and oppressive silence surrounded them. On the largest open wall hung a watercolor print of a mother in a flowy summer dress reading to a child in a hammock. Instead of inspiring tranquility as intended, the art served as a reminder of what was at stake. This body had to be stronger than her last, not only for herself but also for this baby, another innocent brought into a messy romance. Unlike the last, Noah would be a good father. Was Claire's body strong enough to be a mother? Was she?

Thank goodness for reality TV. If not for those labor and

delivery programs, she might have passed out when the doctor wheeled in the ultrasound machine. Millie focused so intently on the ominous black screen that she nearly missed the doctor's name. What truly frightened her was the white plastic wand. Dr. Beamus claimed it would help them see the baby, but it looked more like an alien torture device to her.

Her doctor being a woman lessened the mortification, but that in itself was surprising. Certainly, she had heard of women nurses, but never a doctor. The young doctor's mousey brown ponytail swayed as she looked back and forth between Millie and her machine.

"How far along do you think you are?" asked Dr. Beamus.

Millie blinked rapidly at the pretty doctor, searching for something to say that didn't make her seem like a dimwit or a liar. "I have no idea. I only just found out."

That was the problem with taking over someone else's body; Millie didn't inherit her memories. For all she knew, Claire could have found out this morning or a month ago. There was just no way to tell.

She looked up at Noah, hoping to find reassurance. His face was ashen, and his normally warm blue eyes were cold and blank. Somewhere in the rush to the hospital, he had rolled up his shirtsleeves, pulled his tie askew, and opened the top two buttons of his collared shirt. He held her hand, but his grip was limp and clammy. She squeezed his hand. He returned it, along with a weak smile that did not quite reach his eyes.

It hurt to have him look at her that way—with such detachment—scalding her already raw emotions with burning unshed tears. She had only to open her mouth and spill her secret to change that look. The doubt that he would believe her and still marry her lingered like poison. She had come back for him, for their love. As she worked to undo the damage Claire had done, her purpose would have to be enough to carry her.

Millie focused her attention on the ultrasound screen to avoid thinking about her feet in stirrups and the cold press of plastic—something else she had not counted on. She wanted to scream in panic and struggled against the impulse to scramble backward off the table. She bit down on her bottom lip and watched through a veil of tears as the gray and black static began to settle into a shape that pulsed with a rapid whoosh-whoosh noise.

"Is our baby okay, doctor?" Millie's voice shook with suppressed emotions and fear for the tiny unborn soul that Claire had left in her care. "What is that sound?"

"That's your baby's strong and steady heartbeat." Dr. Beamus smiled at her indulgently. "I would say you are about twelve weeks along. Congratulations."

"Twelve weeks?" Millie and Noah said in unison.

Jerking back away from Millie as though she bit him, Noah's face reddened, and his eyes grew dark as though a storm had rushed in. "How did you miss something like that?"

"I wouldn't worry too much, Mr. McDonough." The doctor said, cutting off any further harsh words. "It happens more often than you think. If she was under enough stress to have caused the asthma attack she had today, she likely just missed the signs."

Noah rubbed the back of his neck, staring at the door as if he wanted to bolt. He took a step towards it, then turned and sat on the lone chair in the furthest corner of the room. There was no argument with the doctor, but his rigid posture and the distance he had put between them spoke volumes.

It seemed unlikely to Millie as well that Claire hadn't known, but it wasn't a sentiment she could express. The baby was okay. That was the important thing. She had to trust that she and Noah would find their way too.

The ultrasound over, the horrible wand was withdrawn. She wished fervently that Noah hadn't seen her violated that way, but if he hadn't been there holding her hand—detached as he was—the whole experience would have been so much worse to endure. The doctor turned off the machine and pulled off her gloves.

"Here let me help you." Dr. Beamus grabbed Millie's arm and helped her sit up with a bright, generic smile plastered on her face. "I would suggest you get some rest, Ms. Jennings. You were fortunate this time."

"More than you know, ma'am."

The doctor gave Millie a confused look and then defaulted back to her smile. "You can get dressed now. Your breathing has stabilized, and you're doing well enough that we don't see any reason to keep you for observation. I'll send the nurse in with your discharge paperwork."

Millie nodded distantly as she heard the door click closed. Her focus was on Noah, stewing in his corner. She opened her mouth to tell him who she was, to take advantage of this time alone with him, but the words refused to come. It made her want to weep.

"I'm sorry." That was all Mille could manage.

Those two words broke the gathering storm behind his eyes. He stood in a rush, knocking the chair to the floor with a clatter that thundered through her battered nerves. She counted with her eyes closed against his outburst, waiting to see just how close the storm would come. When she opened them, he loomed an inch from her face. She leaned away out of reflex.

"What exactly are you sorry for? For hiding this from me or using it to get what you want? Tell me, Claire, because that's what this is about, isn't it?"

Millie flinched at the bitter accusation in his whispered shout and because he was right—just not for the reasons that he assumed. "I'm sorry because I didn't know until today and for the things, I said last night. I came to the house to make you dinner and apologize to you. I love you, and I still want to marry you."

Her heartbeat thumped heavily in her throat, making it difficult to swallow past her own misplaced fears. He was not the man who lashed out at her in anger when he felt trapped. That was another life. When he took a step back from her, as if she had slapped him with her words, she let out the breath she had been holding.

She was apologizing for someone else's actions, but she had no other choice if she couldn't tell him she was Millie, and God how she wanted to say the words. It was cruel that she could be this close and yet locked into silence by some unknown force. She would do her best to show him, but she prayed he would understand soon.

"Were you going to tell me about the baby tonight?" He turned his back on her as if he couldn't look at her while she answered what he assumed would be a lie.

"No. I didn't want you to think that was the only reason I still wanted to marry you because it's not." They were Claire's own words and the truth as far as she had planned.

Noah's head dropped forward, his eyes closed. She watched his hand at his side open and close into a tight fist as he seemed to shake off some thought he didn't wish to share. As much as she hated that silence, she let it stretch. Sometimes it served a greater purpose, and she hoped this was one of those times. She needed him to put the pieces together and for the wedding to continue.

"Get dressed so I can take you home." Noah didn't look at her; he just left her there alone.

chapter 14

millie sat in the same car she had watched back down the driveway every day since Noah had first come to her house. She thought that was where he was taking her until he stopped them in front of an unfamiliar brick building. There were four white doors evenly spaced apart and a large square window beside each one. The unease that had bubbled in her stomach for most of the silent drive had reached a rolling boil that she could no longer ignore.

Clutching Claire's purse to her chest, Millie turned to face Noah. "I thought you were taking me home?"

"Until after our wedding, this is your home." He gaze remained fixed forward, his voice tightly controlled.

Millie wanted to be relieved that he still planned to marry her, that he believed enough of what she said for that to be possible. She just wanted to be with him, not in some strange place, alone. It would be so much easier if the words would leave her lips.

"I was wrong. That house will be our home. You've done so much to make it that way, and I should have been grateful." Claire would never have said that Millie knew, but she had long wanted her to show him the appreciation he deserved.

He turned to look her in the eyes, finally. They were still the flinty blue-gray of storm clouds rather than the clear skies she had known. She fought her own desire to reach out and touch him. Now that she finally could—now that she had held his hand—the need was consuming her. Her grip on the leather bag tightened painfully to keep her hands in compliance, even as she felt her own resolve weaken.

Would he suffer all alone in the house, searching for her? Once again, she fought herself to say the words—to end both their misery. Her mouth opened and closed like a fish gasping for air, but no words came out.

"Do you need your inhaler again?"

"No," she said, forcing down the sob that caught in her throat.

Millie knew she needed the time to learn what she could about Claire so that she might slip into the woman's abandoned life, but the press of his lips last night had been so brief. Her new body leaned forward without her consent, not much but enough to be noticed.

"Did you put in contacts to change your eyes?"

Noah's odd question struck her like a bucket of ice water.

She blinked rapidly and shook her head in answer. "No, why do you ask?"

He reached out, cupping her chin in his callused hands. Millie's breath hitched at the unexpected contact, and she rubbed her cheek into it like a sated cat, causing heat to build in her new body. He tightened his grip. Not enough to hurt, just enough to hold her still. He gazed deep into her eyes, and for a heart-stopping moment, she wondered if he would kiss her. She wanted it desperately, but she wanted him to know he was kissing Millie. Until she found a way to show him, it just couldn't be.

"I must be imagining things." Noah dropped his hands away and sat back. "You should go in. You need to get some rest like the doctor said."

Now that was a problem, she had Claire's keys but had no idea which key to use. Millie's only hope was that he would wonder why she needed take her time trying each one. She learned while filling out paperwork at the hospital that hers was door number two. She sighed heavily, wishing they could just go home. One glanced at Noah's hard expression told her he was not leaving with her.

Giving up, Millie climbed out of the car. As soon as the door clicked closed, he pulled away from the curb. Unable to make herself move, she watched his receding taillights until he turned the corner and was gone. He was probably anxious to get home to Millie, not knowing he had just left her behind.

Standing there on the curb, Millie dug into Claire's purse until she came up with a tiny black compact. Flipping the plastic case open, she ignored the blush and angled the mirror to see her own eyes. She recalled that Claire's eyes had been a pale, frigid blue, fitting for the ice princess image Millie had, but the eyes looking back at her did not resemble that.

They were Millie's own eyes—a sort of hazel gray overlaid with gold, like the sun peeking through the clouds. The windows to her soul had altered to mark the changing of the guard. It was liberating to know that at least something physical was still hers, and standing here alone, it made all the difference.

She couldn't go on staring at herself all day. Whether she wanted to or not, she had to set the next steps of her new life in motion. Heartsore, she was too numb from the day's events to process how she made it from the curb to the door or how many keys she fumbled through before the lock gave and she stumbled inside.

It was a tidy apartment and very different from Noah's oversized bachelor décor. A slim green sofa dominated the space. It reminded her of her mother's formal sofa but without the curves. She decided that with a colorful mix of pillows, she would probably like it. Bare as it currently was of anything comfortable, only its color spoke to its owner's personality. Most of the place was like that, she discovered: beautiful and artful but lacking anything cozy and relaxed to give it balance.

Millie wandered from room to room, peeking in drawers and cabinets for information. Somehow, she had to live this life and show Noah she wasn't Claire. Millie needed any clue to tell her how to do it: where she worked, the wedding, anything.

The bedroom was where she found it. It was where Claire truly lived—at least that's how it appeared. It was still as clean as the rest of the place, but layers of inviting pillows covered the bed, more than just the requisite pair. Unlike the vibrant colors in the public spaces, Claire had chosen a simple pallet of creams and white, monochromatically layered throughout. On the nightstand sat a binder overflowing with papers and a journal.

Millie picked up the binder and ran her fingers over the gold embossed lettering on the white linen cover—Wedding Planner. Flipping through the pages, she was amazed at every meticulous detail, from the overinflated budget to the schedule of every part and piece for the next week. No detail was too small for Claire's meticulous documentation.

Millie was relieved. She never expected others to be as organized as she was herself, but in the present circumstance, it would alleviate much of the pressure. She was also shocked when she read over the budget. This wedding was costing them $50,000. Such a sum was outrageous and no doubt much of it had come out of Noah's budget for the house.

Just thinking of him made her heart ache. How was she going to get through to Noah? Tidy as Claire was, the woman's life was a mess of manipulation. What would he believe? Millie sat on the edge of the bed and looked down at the binder in her lap.

This was her life now, and things were going to change. Maybe then, he would see.

chapter 15

five days of maddening silence had passed since Noah felt her trembling lips kiss him. Five days since Millie had stumbled out of the kitchen shaken and diminished because he begged her to try—God forgive him.

He left the TV on for her every day, but no change. Noah was sorely tempted to open the attic door and enter her space. Fear that she was gone forever held him in check. He wasn't ready to confront that possibility.

Instead, he sat in the hallway slumped with his back against the door, waiting for her to emerge. He had functioned on a loop of work, crying in front of the attic door, sleeping on the floor in front of the attic door, and work again. His five o'clock shadow had moved on to a full-fledged beard. He wouldn't have eaten if Claire had not brought him something every evening.

His life was undergoing a seismic shift. All he wanted was to wait here for Millie, but Claire had inserted herself at every opportunity. She had been like a different person since he found her on the kitchen floor—loving and less critical. Moreover, her sudden interest in the house was raising questions in his mind that made no sense.

The day after he drove her home from the hospital, she went to the library and brought him copies of articles on the family that had built the house—Millie's family. Unwilling to drive since the asthma attack, she took a cab to get there. It was so unlike her to go out of her way or to show any fear of something as ordinary as driving. Claire brazened her way through life, something he had initially liked about her, and now she seemed timid—like Millie.

Noah sat with the file spread out on the floor next to him. Mildred Standish—that was the name in the obituary had been married, buried a child, and died all in the same year. Her gentle spirit had endured all of that, just as she claimed. She had missed her brother going off to fight in the Second World War and his premature death in a nearby town. Her parents had even died in this house. What must that have been like for her? To watch her parents and siblings carry on without her?

Now he would betray Millie with Claire because of the baby. He just wanted to explain it to Millie before it happened. When the doctor told them the baby would be fine, the wonder and love that appeared to fill Claire while she gripped his hand was so contrary to what he had been prepared for. He loved Claire before—or thought he had, and made this innocent life with her. He had to try. He just didn't want to.

"Noah?" This new softer version of Claire's voice drifted up the stairs.

He heard the door click shut, and her light footfalls on the stairs. As the top of her head and her eyes came into view, he could almost swear he was looking at Millie. Their wheat blonde hair had been the same, but he recalled Claire's eyes as a pale blue. Now they looked like they had been shot through with sunshine. Hadn't Millie's been like that?

She came into full view, dismissing his fanciful wish that it would be Millie in the flesh rather than Claire. "I thought I'd find you here." Her tone held no malice or judgement, just a sad observation tinged with empathy.

"Got nowhere else to be." Noah sat the articles aside that he already read at least a hundred times and let his hands rest limp on his raised knees.

Not so long ago that would have sparked an argument, but now it was as if she knew what was wrong. Claire lowered herself to sit on the top step, across from him. She tucked the light floral fabric of her dress around her legs as if to preserve her already tattered modesty. This, too, was a change in her.

Claire had gone from form-fitting clothing and high-heels to comfortable loose dresses belted at her still tiny waist and flat shoes. The artfully applied makeup was gone. She looked younger and softer somehow, like a summer goddess that should be frolicking in fields of flowers and sunshine rather than lurking in the offices of corporate America.

"I brought you something." Claire pulled a dog-eared envelope from her purse.

With her eyes downcast demurely and a small smile spreading across her face, she slid it across the floor to him. "I wish it was more, but it was too late to make more changes and get refunds."

Noah picked up the envelope and peeked inside. Cash. He thumbed through the stack of fifties and hundreds. There was at least ten grand here.

"Where did you get this?" He asked his tone incredulous.

"First I sold that couture wedding gown, along with the veil and tiara. It fit her style more than mine, and it cost a small fortune." She looked at her hands instead of him as though she was shy about her actions. "That was about half of it. I bought an off-the-rack dress instead. I like it so much better."

He couldn't believe what he was hearing—her style? What was that supposed to mean?

"I also talked to the caterer. We didn't really need three meat options or individual plate service. I saved a lot scaling it back to family style and just having one meat. I would have changed the photographer and the venue, too, but you guys were under contract, so it was too late." She blushed and met Noah's gaze. Pride radiated from her as she continued. "I want you to use the money I recouped on the house."

Listening to Claire speak, you would think she was talking about someone else making decisions, but she had made each one. None of it added up. She didn't talk like herself, dress like herself, act like herself. It was as if someone ripped Claire out and another, better version had stepped inside.

"Noah, are you okay?"

He nodded, struck mute by the idea. Could that really have happened?

Claire stood up, leaving her purse where she dropped it and walked to him. "Come on. You've been on the floor all week. Your muscles must ache." She held her hand out to him. "You need a hot bath and a shave."

Noah stared up at those beautiful eyes. There was something about them that he just could not say no to. They were the key to unraveling all of this, he was sure of it. Noah put his hand in Claire's and allowed her to steady him as he climbed up off the floor.

Hand in hand, she led him down the hall, through the bedroom into the now finished bathroom. "I'm so glad you stuck to your guns about this bathroom. It's lovely and she really didn't need a bigger closet."

There it was again—referring to herself in the third person and that she would bring up the closet. It was as if she were laying out a bread trail for him to follow with every new statement. He thought back over each conversation they had. Not the day of her asthma attack but after, and yes, she had gone back and forth between first and third person.

While he ruminated on the possibilities, she left him standing in the middle of the white tiled bathroom. He watched Claire, hungry for something, some new sign as she balanced on the edge of the tub, running him a bath. Steamrolled up from the porcelain, caressing and circling her as though she were on display. When she looked back at him, his breath caught. Could it really be Millie looking back at him? Or was it just his lonely heart wishing?

His eyes never left hers as he pulled off his shirt and shucked his slacks to the floor. He stepped out of them and walked to her. Her hand was over her heart and heat had risen in her cheeks as though she had never seen him nude. Claire, of course, had—but Millie, shy and reserved Millie had not and would have blushed.

"Let me get your razor, and I'll shave you while you're in the tub." Her voice was breathless as she said it.

She moved to the sink. While he sank down into the water, allowing it to soothe the cramps out of his muscles, he watched her toe off her shoes. She opened the cabinet and retrieved his razor, shaving cream, and a glass she then filled with water.

Claire set her supplies down on the floor next to the tub, turned off his water, and pulled the stool over from the wall. She settled in behind him and with a deft touch, lathered his scruffy face was shaving cream. She wet the blade in her cup of water and made the first stroke across his cheek.

"I do admire the tub she chose. I can at least give her that much credit, but the rest of this room is your amazing work." Her hands were quick and sure as she shaved away his beard and then cleaned the blade in her glass.

Her touch eased the tension in his neck and shoulders but built it lower. As she smoothed away the gruff edges of his sorrow, he was almost sure it was Millie. It would explain so much. He just needed something to seal it, some final sign—if she would only say it.

When she finished his shave, she loomed over him from her seat behind him and whispered, "You brought my home back to life."

He caught her thin wrist as he pulled her around in front of him so that he could look into her shining eyes again. "You're in there aren't you?"

Tears welled in her eyes, and she dropped the razor, sending it clattering to the floor. She worried her bottom lip between her teeth, but she didn't deny it. Her free hand moved to his now smooth cheek, stroking it.

Noah let go of her wrist and framed her dainty face in his large hands. "I've missed you."

"I never left."

Noah pulled her half over him until her mouth crashed into his. She didn't kiss with the confidence that he knew with Claire. She kissed with the shy sweetness he had only known from Millie's lips. She branded it into his memory with perfect clarity five nights ago.

chapter 16

Millie was breathless with the intensity of her gratitude. She still couldn't tell him, but somehow he knew. She had chosen her words to him carefully, and her reward was falling into bliss with the only man she had ever truly loved.

This kiss was so much more than the first had been. The intensity of feeling without the veil of death between them was an awakening that set her new body on fire with need. The feeling pooled in her center as he invaded her mouth with his, stoking the embers of her desire with his tongue.

Noah pulled her into the tub with him so that she sat his lap, apparently forgetting that unlike him, she was still fully clothed. Water sloshed onto the floor with the sudden movement. His fingers met hers at the leather belt around her waist. They fumbled at it together as his lips moved down the column of her neck. When the buckle gave, he flung the leather across the room and moved his hands to the soaked hem of her dress, pushing it up her thighs.

Millie relaxed in the caress of his wandering hands, pulling the wet material up her body, inch by delicious inch. She didn't suffer any of the revulsion that she remembered, no distracted fear. There were no memories dogging her in this moment. It was only the two of them—at last. Even so, when he pulled the dress over her head, she crossed her arms over the front of her bra, self-consciousness a last vestige of her old fashion modesty.

He tossed the dress aside as he had the belt. "Honey, don't hide from me ever again—please." His voice cracked with emotion—relief from the pain that she caused for the reward of this moment and so many others.

"I promise," she whispered, her own voice shaking.

Noah covered her trembling hands as she released the front clasp on her bra. Emboldened, she let the straps slide off her shoulders and over the edge of the tub. Her cheeks flushed with heat, but she didn't hide. Instead, she gripped his arms as one of Noah's hands covered her bare breast. He stroked and rolled the sensitized peak. Her breath caught with the flood of sensation—a distraction from his other hand as it moved to her panties, drawing them down her legs.

The last physical barrier between them gone, she shifted in the water from her position sitting across his lap to straddle his body. Noah groaned as her folds stroked his hard length without entering her. Leaning forward, he took the tip of her other breast in his mouth as his hand continued to work the first.

Millie's body felt like it had three burning points, her achy breasts and the pulsing need between her legs, connected intimately to him. He suckled and caressed them as she rocked against him. Taking ownership her own pleasure like this—the build-up—it overwhelmed her senses bringing her to a peak so bright she thought the light had come back for her because surely nothing short of heaven could be that good.

Millie cried out with her release and collapsed against Noah's chest. His hands moved to run lazily down her spine, stroking up and down to calm her. The tenderness brought tears to her eyes. Without his own completion, he was tending to her, making her feel treasured. The experience moved her, deep down, where she now knew her soul lived.

"Are you ready, love?" The pet name, the intimacy of his whisper against her skin sent a ripple of renewed desire through her—like a soft echo of the climax she just had.

She nodded against his chest, still unable to speak.

With gentle strength, Noah lifted her, not much but enough to position himself at her opening. Millie moved down, the length of him slowly filling her up, stretching her in ways that had never felt so good or so right. This body might be familiar with him, but Millie was not. He knew—God bless him, Noah knew who it was he was making love to whether he said it or not. It was in the care he took with her as he moved, allowing her to adjust until he was fully sheathed inside of her. Even then, he paused. In that moment when their bodies connected, it seemed as if they were bound body and soul. He held her still, allowing her to get used to him—to revel in it.

Their eyes met. His cloudless blues brimmed with his own watery tears to match her own. They had both suffered so much to get to this moment—to feel one another. It was a miracle of epic proportions. God had not forsaken her, as she believed so long ago.

Unfamiliar with this position her movements were tentative as she rocked in a slow rhythm with her hips. It was equal parts exquisite and torture. As if she were running towards some precipice that she couldn't fathom. His mouth found hers in the madness, and she melted into him. His hands moved to her hips, helping her as they moved in tandem with their heartbeats.

Their bodies crushed together, every impact of their slippery flesh sent a shockwave of sensation through the already stimulated bundle of nerves above where they joined. She felt the end looming up ahead, and she wanted him to tumble with her—needed it. He must have felt it, too, because he began controlling their pace, bucking beneath her and urging her hips to move faster. None of the urgency of their lovemaking lessened the connection she felt between their souls—if anything it grew with their impending climax.

He claimed another kiss from her lips that mirrored her own desperation. When she felt him shudder and heard him moan into their kiss, her own release rushed up and took her down with him. They clung to one another, shaking in the cooling water, a swirling raw nerve of intensity that pulsed through them both until it slowed and ebbed away.

He released her mouth, and she rubbed her cheek against his smooth one. "I love you, Noah."

She wanted to hear him say her name—her real one, and the only piece that would take the moment from beautiful to perfect. His actions showed her he knew her identity, but the little insecure voice that needled her heart wanted the visceral confirmation.

Millie lay against him, waiting and basking in the aftershocks of their lovemaking. The cool water lapped at her sensitized skin, and she shivered.

Noah's hooded gaze met hers. "I'm not taking care of you, am I?"

He raised up out of the water, lifting her with him and causing the water to slosh inside the porcelain. He sat her down on shaking legs on the cold tile floor and then climbed out after her. Grabbing a folded white towel on the shelf beside them, he wrapped her in the fluffy terry cloth, rubbing her with it and warming her limbs. He wrapped a second one around his own waist. Then he lifted her once more and carried her out to the bedroom.

Millie felt like the bride she was about to be for the second time and truly couldn't wait to make it official. If one day could be like this, she couldn't wait to start on forever. Noah laid her on the bed and climbed over her. Leaning down, he parted the towel at her belly.

"You found a way, didn't you? You said I deserved a family and were so sure you couldn't give me one, but here you are." Noah placed a chaste kiss on her bare flesh, over the child in her womb.

He was saying the right things, melting her heart with each word. What he wasn't saying whispered at her, building her self-doubt.

She lifted his chin, gently until his blue eyes met hers. "I want to hear you say my name."

Noah rolled away from her. His silence answered for him. If he were certain, she knew in her heart that he would have said it, he would have freed them both.

Mille worried her bottom lip, struggling to choke back the tears that threatened, like the storm she saw returning to his eyes. She rolled off the bed, leaving him there. There weren't any clothes yet in her custom closet, so she went to his. She unearthed the gray t-shirt he had been wearing the day he moved into her house and a pair of shorts. Grasping the towel tightly, she scuttled past him into the bathroom to retrieve her shoes. She abandoned her soggy dress and underthings and dressed quickly in the borrowed clothes.

When she came back out, he was sitting up on the bed watching her. "Where are you going?"

She tried again, opening her mouth to tell him she was Millie. Like every other time, nothing came out. What had happened between them had been poignant, and had altered her irrevocably, but it was not enough. She was certain now. He had to believe it, or she would never be free to say it. Whatever force in the universe had given her this second chance had imposed a cruel limit which threatened to break them apart.

"I'm going to call a cab. I'll see you on Saturday." Millie left the room but stopped at the top of the stairs. She called back to him. "Let me know when you believe. I'll wait as long as it takes."

chapter 17

noah stood in front of the church, clasping hands with Claire as the Pastor spoke. Each word in the ceremony felt like a death knoll for his battered heart. He reached up to tug at his tux, slipping his fingers between the collar and his skin to relieve the pressure. It brought to mind a marital noose growing ever tighter.

Ultimately, Claire hadn't brought him here—that tiny heartbeat had. He couldn't forget the panic in Claire's eyes when she told him about the baby and the relief that chased it away when they had done the ultrasound. It put him in this moment.

He still couldn't find Millie, and he was wracked with guilt over what he had done with Claire. He allowed his grief to play a cruel trick on him and found peace in a lie. He wanted to believe it was Millie he had made love to, but he wasn't sure. When he looked at her, it was as if his longing for Millie superimposed her on Claire. It was unnerving the response it brought on him.

Their vows were spoken, the rings exchanged, but his heart ached. He couldn't turn off his feelings for Millie. How else could he have deluded himself into believing she had possessed Claire? But something was off there. She was so different and the look in her eyes when he refused to say her name had been like a deep wound. He didn't know what to make of it.

More importantly, he loved Millie, and here he stood betraying her by marrying Claire. When Claire had come down the aisle, it moved him to tears, not by love for his bride, but with longing for the spirit, he envisioned in her place. Her new gown came past her knees but well above her ankle. The lace sleeves gave it modesty, and the fascinator instead of a veil made it seem vintage—more like something Millie would have chosen, not Claire.

The echoes he saw of the woman he loved were gutting him and breaking more than his heart. With the visions of her everywhere, it wouldn't be long before his mind broke too.

Music cued up, and they moved together behind the altar. Noah's hand shook as he lifted his candle to meet Claire's, lighting their unity candle. Then the marriage license. He studied Claire's face as she signed. The soft upturn of her lips into a shy smile seemed so unlike her, so demure. He felt a stab of guilt for his own melancholy on a day that was supposed to mean so much.

He picked up the pen and scrawled his own name beside hers, then froze. In his preoccupation, he nearly missed it—her signature. The pastor had warned her during the rehearsal, sign it as she meant to go on because that would be her name when it was done. She had nearly come unglued, she was so happy about the simple warning.

In swirling feminine script—Mildred Claire McDonough.

Noah straightened, his eyes wide with his own shock. In black and white letters, he finally caught on to what her eyes had been trying to tell him since the panic on the kitchen floor. Her smile spread as his own began to take shape.

His addled mind turned over every word, every look between them in the last week. God—she must have been so afraid, and he hadn't made it any easier. He had been cruel on the first day, consumed by his own bitterness. Later, he had been correct in the hallway when her words started to fit into place. When they made love, all she wanted was for him to call her Millie and he had doubted. Why hadn't she told him?

The droning voice of the pastor finally paused, and Noah dragged his mind back to the moment, given more importance than it would have had the moment before.

"You may kiss your bride," the pastor decreed.

Noah reached up, framing her face with his hands as he had the other night. This was too much like his dreams to be the truth, even for a man who could see ghosts.

"Noah, I'm sorry I can't say it. I need for you to know, I'm proud to be your wife."

He searched her eyes, not the frigid blue, but gray and gold like the sun chasing away the clouds. Her eyes looked back at him with adoration. Claire had never looked at him that way.

"How do you know that name?" Noah whispered.

The pastor cleared his throat expectantly, but the bride paid him no mind.

"I came to be with you, for the rest of this life," she answered, "I love you."

It was all he needed to hear. "I love you, Millie McDonough."

The Claire he proposed to would have been mortified to make these people wait, but not his Millie—He kissed her reverently, joy welling up in him. In this moment, he didn't care how or why. There would be time for answers later.

That he could bring her home would be enough.

epilogue

$\mathbf{m}$ille held up the soft white onesie proclaiming, "somebunny loves me". Tears filled her eyes. So many second chances. A second chance at life, love, and now motherhood. For all the hatred she once felt for Claire, it was her that she owed for all of this. It may have been an act of cowardice, but it had been a blessing for her and Noah. She kissed the tiny item of clothing, inhaling the scent of clean laundry and baby powder deeply—committing the precious scent to memory. God only knows how long this chance would last. She made it a point to savor every second of it and took nothing for granted if she could help it.

She laid the tiny article of clothing over her protruding belly, smoothing it down and rocking slightly as if she was holding and rocking the baby on the outside—soon enough.

A creak in the hardwood floors that her and Noah had saved and painstakingly refinished had her smiling seconds before his arms wrapped around her. Noah's rough hands laid over her own, his thumbs making soothing circles that mirrored the ones she made where the baby now kicked.

"How is my love feeling today?" The low rumble of his voice and the heat of his breath on her neck sent a thrill through places that made her blush.

"Our little one seems to be happy and active today." She willfully ignored his meaning. "I just wanted to put the last of his baby clothes away." She said *his* but he or she—they never did find out. All that mattered was that their child was healthy, even if she couldn't help but believe the baby would be a boy.

Noah slowly spun her around to face him, as though they had been dancing. Then he pulled her into his body as near as her heavily pregnant body allowed, until they were doing just that—slow dancing to a song that wasn't playing. He did things like this frequently. It was as if the house that was once so alive for her still was for him. He never mentioned it, but sometimes she wondered what he heard and saw echoing in these walls. Or maybe it was nothing. Just Noah, being his romantic self— something that made her second marriage a happy one thus far.

"While I do love our child, I think you know I meant you." He rocked with her, his hands working the ache in the small of her back as they danced despite the beach ball shape at the front of her. She was just that petite, and he was just that large. "Why is it you seem to always forget about yourself?"

"I don't forget. I'm very aware of myself in fact. Hard not to be."

Noah shook his head, and his eyes grew dark, but she no longer feared the storm of emotion they implied. "I still can't believe you let me say the awful things I did to you."

Millie reached up and pulled him down to her level. Even so, she had to go up on her toes—something she only felt comfortable doing because of the way he currently held her. She brushed her lips against his. "You didn't know." She repeated her action. "And I couldn't tell you. Although I was proud of how close you came on your own."

That, at last, earned her a smile. "Not as proud as I am of how you made me understand. Now, how are you today, sweetheart?"

She opened her mouth to answer, but the wave of pain that rolled through her stomach muscles stole her words. Her breath came out in a whoosh instead. Her fingers dug into Noah's arms.

"Millie?"

When it passed, and she could speak again, she forced a strained smile as she looked up seeing the concern in his gray-blue eyes. She always focused there on his soul. "It's nothing. Just a Braxton Hicks, the doctor, told me about. That one was just a little strong, but they've been happening today."

He continued to rub her back even though they had stopped moving. "When was the last one?" Bless him, he tried to keep his tone light and the concern absent, but he wasn't very good at it—not with her anyway.

She laid her head on his arm, relaxing into him. "About ten minutes before you came in here." That seemed to satisfy Noah, and they started to move again. "Wait—now I have to pee."

Noah chuckled, and she stepped back from the circle of his arms. As she did, a sudden wet feeling made tears sting in her eyes. "Damn it."

His brows went up at her curse. She had done it so

infrequently, but really, peeing on yourself in front of your husband was mortifying. The whole course of this pregnancy she had never lost control like this. She tried to waddle from the room, but more wetness ran down her thighs with each step, soaking her socks. At least she was wearing a dress—nothing else fit at this point.

"Honey—I think your water broke." As he spoke, another contraction rolled through her as if to drive home the point. That was much too soon to be a coincidence.

Millie reached out to grab the doorframe and steady herself, but she wasn't close enough and began to tumble forward. However, Noah was there. He took her outstretched hand and steadied her.

"Let's get you down to the car."

She looked back at the white and yellow nursery they had been dancing in seconds before. "I'm not ready."

He kissed her forehead, smoothing back her hair as he waited for her legs to be steady enough to move. "He's operating on his own schedule, honey."

Millie's legs shook, and she tried to step forward but ended up sliding down towards the floor instead.

"Nope, I've got you." He scooped her up in his arms as though she were nothing more than the ethereal body she had once been instead of the bloated whale she currently felt like. She didn't resist, just circled her arms around his neck and rested her head against his chest. "Let's get you down to the car."

***

"One last push and you get to meet your new baby."

Someone, namely Millie's husband, needed to read her mind and tell that nurse to stop with her false promises.

The pain was so much more searing than before. Her son, who came too early all those decades ago, had merely slipped from her body while she fought to hold him in. This time, she struggled to help the infant leave her. This experience had her doing something she hadn't done in ages. It had her praying, but not to God—to Claire—the woman who hadn't wanted this moment, who had given it over to her.

In her own mind, she whispered, *Claire, if you can hear me. Help me bring our child into this world.* It was a simple prayer, but there wasn't time for more. Millie had already been pushing for over an hour, and these contractions were on top of each other. She didn't have much more to give, even in this body that was so much stronger than her previous one had been—asthma and all.

Someone put an oxygen mask over her face, and she felt the start of the next contraction roll down her stomach and sides.

"Wait, Millie, don't push yet." The doctor started to turn away.

Her mother's remembered words drifted through her mind as if they had floated to her from the past. *Trust your body. It knows what to do and when.*

"No, now!" Millie commanded and rolled forward, bearing down as she had been doing with each push before.

This time there was more there as if she wasn't doing it alone. It was as if something reached through her and pushed down from the inside, forcing the infant through her resisting body.

The doctor turned in time and caught the child's head. The rest was a blur in her exhausted state, as the shoulders slipped free along with the rest of the babe.

"Congratulations. It's a boy."

Of course, he was. She had somehow known he would be. Millie looked at Noah with tear-filled eyes, and he nodded his approval.

To her, he whispered, "I'm so proud of you." To the nurse and anyone else who cared to listen he announced, "His name is Benjamin."

The nurse rested the now swaddled and messy baby on her chest as she sobbed with happiness that she hadn't experienced with her first son. "Thank you." She meant more than just for the name. There would always be moments where this baby would have been her lost little Ben, now he really could be. No amount of the therapy she was doing could make that go away. Now he had given her another way she could heal from it. They could.

Noah brushed the baby's brow, the way he often did hers and kissed the newborn's temple as he smiled back at Millie. "No, sweetheart, thank you."

the end

playlist

I make it no secret that music is a heavy influence in my writing. It sets the mood for my imaginary world and each book calls for something different. This list evolved over time, rewrites and the like to what you see now. If you're interested, you can find a link on my website to a video playlist on YouTube. Enjoy the mood music and a window into what drove me for Millie and Noah's love story.

Dust to Dust – Civil Wars

Magic – Cold Play

I've Got This Friend – Civil Wars

Breathe Me – Sia

Ghosts That We Know – Mumford & Sons

Tell Me True – Sarah Jarosz

White Blank Page – Mumford & Sons

Falling In Love At A Coffee Shop – Landon Pigg

Paper Bag – Fiona Apple

Awake My Soul – Mumford & Sons

Precious Illusions (Acoustic Version) – Alanis Morissette

Lover Of The Light – Mumford & Sons

sneak peek

By all rights, Seth should only have one thing on his mind: scare them off.

He didn't much like the look of the first two. The small one with the austere black hair was definitely a skeptic, and the colorful one looked tough. He had seen their kind before. They came with their scientific instruments, intent to prove to the world that every haunting was just misunderstood natural occurrences. It made them harder to convince to run, but it was a game he hadn't lost yet.

Through the years, it had taken him time to refine his scare tactics. The tools in his arsenal ranged from disembodied voices to moving objects. The only line he chose not to cross was violence, especially when those he chased off where of the female persuasion.

The key was to find a target who would make the others believe. The redhead who pranced around like a nervous spaniel would do nicely. Too bad he couldn't bring himself to use her like that. When he was alive, she was just the sort of girl next door he would have mooned over. Hell, he was doing it now.

There was something about her. Whatever it was, it halted his usual determination to wallow in misery. It might have been her timid approach to his front porch or the way she ran in through the front door because of its settling groan. Or it may have been that her auburn curls reminded him of autumn leaves and her amber eyes glowed like apple cider that once warmed his body in the same way that her skittish gaze warmed his soul. He may not welcome the intrusion, but dead didn't make him immune to her physical charms. It just left him without the means to make them lead anywhere useful.

He followed her as she moved around the table, gingerly

perusing the instruments that her friends believed would reveal his presence.

"Tell me your name, beautiful."

"Amanda, I've got camera one and two set up where we talked about. Bettina, would you like to come with me while I take some base EMF readings?" The blue-haired girl poked her head around the doorframe from the kitchen.

Loud modern colors aside, the blue-haired friend reminded him of the women painted on the sides of the planes he had occasionally seen on base—harmless reminders of home meant to keep the boys happy.

His gaze followed hers, interested to see which one would respond and conveniently provide his answer. When the little one draped in black looked up from her screen, Seth grumbled his disappointment.

"Go with Charity and she can show you how we do things." From her answer, he assumed the one hiding behind the laptop must be Amanda.

"Um—sure, why not." His red head looked between her two friends before continuing. "What do you need me to do?"

Bettina. He turned the name over in his mind as he watched her stroke the side of her flannel covered arms as if to ward off a chill. His gaze slid down her body, taking in the way her oversized flannel shirt grazed the tops of her thighs. The uniqueness of her name suited her equally distinctive beauty.

"Grab an IR camera and come on," Charity ordered.

Bettina looked down again at the table full of equipment and frowned.

Amanda reached over and picked up a device, shoving it at Bettina. "This one."

"Oh—thanks." She took the camera, a shy smile quirked up the corner of her full lips. "You guys are going to have to be more specific with me for a while."

Charity moved into the room and grabbed another device off the table, along with a flashlight. "You follow me with the camera on and I'll take the readings. We can start in the basement, and I'll explain things to you as I go."

Flipping open the tiny screen, Bettina nodded and together the women started towards the back of the house. Charity moved like a cat. Based on the saunter and sway of her hips she was secure in herself. In contrast, Bettina moved more like a timid mouse, trying to sneak away from the cat without notice.

Seth took a moment to enjoy the view Bettina offered before following. Black cotton leggings clung to the prettiest legs he had seen in years. Bettina wore them tucked into worn leather boots that came up to her knees and hugged just as tightly as the leggings. The fashion of this decade really was an improvement. It would be a shame to hide all that under the layers of a loose skirt.

If he still lived, she would be enticement enough to turn on the charm, something he never felt the need to do after the war and his recovery in Paris. No, he had been obsessed with something else.

Seth had been wallowing in his anger for so long that he had nearly forgotten what it felt like. Maybe, she could stay a little while. It was nice not to feel that burden of anger hanging on his every step, like the chains that Jacob Marley brandished in *A Christmas Carol.* He had built that chain link by link though the last years of his short life.

Their silent passage to the back of the house ended with

the squeal of hinges that hadn't been oiled since he had successfully driven out the last owners of this house. Bettina shifted nervously behind her friend, device open and pointed over Charity's shoulder to peek into the darkness ahead.

Charity traipsed down the stairs as if dank old basements were nothing to worry over.

His girl approached the open door as if it was a gaping mouth intent to swallow her. She took a deep breath and threw herself into the inky oblivion. The rapid thud of her footfalls racing down the stairs echoed up at him.

Seth chuckled to himself as he followed. He located her in the darkness through the glow of flashlights and her rapid panting. Someone should tell her that if she didn't stop hyperventilating she would faint.

Having found her, this was as far as he could bring himself to wait before he touched her. Just a light touch, stroking the back of her shaking hand. He could say she needed the comfort but he would only be lying to himself. A selfish need to feel contact, muted though it was, drove his actions.

A sharp indrawn breath punctuated Bettina's still rapid breathing.

Her friend swung the flashlight up at Bettina's face. "You gonna make it, Red?"

Bettina slowed her breathing by small increments, but he could see her shaking like those autumn leaves her hair resembled, clinging for purchase in the wind. "I'll be fine. Don't let me keep you from what you need to do."

No scream. Seth had expected more from a woman who seemed terrified by every step she took. But with cobwebs hanging from the floor joists above them, she may have discounted it as nothing.

Making her scream hadn't been the point of the contact anyway, and that should have sent him back up the stairs away from her. No good could come from this fascination with her. After all of that, there was only tingling in his fingers; he hadn't really felt her at all.

"You just need a distraction." Charity's voice was buoyant in the darkness. Clearly, she was in her element. "Have you ever watched one of those ghost hunting shows that talked about EMFs, EVPs--that kinda thing?"

Bettina shook her head in the darkness, sighed and then answered aloud, "Not really."

"That's okay, I can fill in the gaps. I just didn't want to tell you things you already had a handle on." Charity paused to scan a pipe with her meter and then continued on her circuit of the utilitarian space. "EMF stands for electromagnetic field and is man-made. So the point of what I'm doing is to establish what's normal for this house, before we stir anything up by asking questions."

"You've already stirred something up," Seth said, although he knew they couldn't hear. Sometimes he just needed the sound of his own voice to stave off his impending madness. It hovered over him in the endless tedium like a storm about to break.

Charity continued on her lecture. "Later if we observe a spike or a sudden drop we look for a reason. Sometimes it's a light switch got turned on, but other times—let's just say when we review the footage, we find something."

"Do you guys usually find changes?" Bettina's voice squeaked her question, like a mouse afraid to hear about the cat next door.

Charity shrugged, continuing to wander. "Not everywhere we go and this is the first time we've been able to get in here. Probably the last time too. Still don't know how Amanda pulled that one off. Been trying to get in here forever it seems like."

Hanging on every word, Seth pulled it apart for anything useful. He may have wanted them gone before, but now the idea that this could be their only time here chilled his already icy veins. He was just getting used to the idea that he could like having someone here, especially Bettina. That she would leave—that just couldn't stand.

Seth reached for Bettina again, like a child stroking a favorite blanket for comfort. This time he stroked the blossom of her cheek, gliding his hand across her face and then lifting the curtain of her dark red hair to one side.

Her spine straightened and she glanced up, her eyes scanning the exposed joists above them. "Charity," she whispered. "Something is touching me."

DO YOU LIKE ROMANCE THAT WILL MAKE YOU HOWL?

CHECK OUT THE USHERS RUN PACK BY CASSIE LEIGH

Home For The Howliday
Available now from Broken Typewriter Press. Also available in Audio book.

He may have given up the prize fighting, but he's in for the fight of his life…
Walking away from his wolf pack duties and the woman he loved was the hardest thing Gunner Thoren ever did. Now, ten years later the successful MMA fighter is giving up the cage, and reclaiming what's always been his. Will the howliday season help him win back his mate in time for Christmas?

Turn the page for a sneak peek.

The sultry croon of "Santa Baby" blaring through the crowded cabin might as well have been nails on a chalkboard to Gunner Thoren. The eggnog and holiday cookie smorgasbord only added to his irritation. For the hundredth time he questioned his motivation for coming back into the fold. He'd walked away from a good thing in Las Vegas, to return home to the wolf-pack town of Ushers Run, Iowa. *"Eventually you all come home."* Gunner shook the pack-elder's voice from his already crowded mind. He'd met with the old man along with the pack-leader, Ambrose. It was a lofty position for his best friend to ascend to in Gunner's absence. Then Ambrose blindsided him with a compulsory invitation to attend the festivities this evening. It was intended for the younger members. Some crap about pack bonding.

Gunner just wanted to enjoy being in nature. It was the only part of being home that he looked forward to after a decade of self-imposed exile. The bright lights of Las Vegas lacked a forest for his wolf to run in. Wolves didn't belong skulking through back alleys and desert landscapes. At least Ambrose picked a nice spot in the woods for the cabin he'd designed for the pack's use. Too bad it was currently being overrun with someone's bastardized idea of Christmas cheer.

From his spot in the corner, Gunner sneered at the garish holiday sweaters covered in ice skating reindeer and penguins decorating evergreen trees. The pack he was born to, or at least this generation of it, might be happy to prance around like drunken fools, but he wouldn't be caught dead participating in such stupidity. His brother, Asher, loped toward him from across the room in the easy way that came with overstimulated youth. Battery-powered twinkle lights wrapped around the kid's snowflake-covered sweater. It must have come out of their grandmother's closet.

Asher grinned up at him. "You aren't in party gear, bro!"

Gunner growled and hunkered down in his corner, unwilling to acknowledge the fool. This kid was why he gave up fighting and the title shot he had worked for years to achieve. Now he would run his family's business—the local gym. With their father's passing, his mother needed the help keeping it from going under and his kid brother from tearing down half the town with his idiocy. Less than two years until he graduated and Gunner could take off again. He was already counting down the days.

"Never fear," Asher said, undaunted by Gunner's stoicism. "I knew it would happen, so I brought an extra."

Asher slapped his brother's back and gave him an ineffective shove that left the kid rubbing the sting out of his hand. Gunner stood still as a mountain, which he was as a middleweight fighter. He fought at 185 pounds but walked around closer to 220 between fights.

"Nothing's wrong with my sweater," Gunner groused. He'd worn a normal sweater, a traditional Scandinavian pattern in grey and navy. A respectable sweater, not some castoff thrift store reject.

"You're not getting into the spirit," Asher said, his tone sullen and accusatory.

Feminine laughter that was equal parts wicked and ethereal rose above the chaotic jumble of voices and crappy Christmas pop-music. Gunner tuned out the useless prattle that continued to dump out of his brother's mouth, searching for the owner of that laugh as if it was a homing beacon meant to draw him in.

"You've got enough for both of us." Gunner answered his brother to stop the distracting noise. He searched the nameless faces. The laughter had stopped but he knew he hadn't imagined its siren song.

That's when Gunner saw her. The reason he left town in the first place—Noelle Hiver. She moved like a Nordic goddess come to life—a young and beautiful version of the Norns—as she stood in front of a tinsel-draped tree talking with her hands as if they were weaving a tapestry to illustrate her words. The multicolored lights that reflected off the metallic decorations shone on her like a rainbow spotlight.

The little vixen was a dangerous temptation. Her white sweater dress embroidered with silver poinsettias hugged her lithe curves in places he knew his eyes shouldn't linger—but he couldn't stop himself, just like before. No one should look at the pack-leader's half-sister that way, not if he wanted to keep his eyes. His illicit gaze continued the treacherous journey north to wild platinum blonde hair that skimmed her slender shoulders. He wanted a closer look, perilous as it was. He needed to know if she still wore feathers braided in the riotous curls.

Noelle again laughed at something her companion said, a woman who didn't exist as far as Gunner was concerned, and it rang like bells calling him home. She glanced his way and his heart nearly stopped. Those eyes, guarded aquamarine glaciers, bored into him from across the room and he was curious what the pack abomination had made of herself.

He'd never called her that, but nearly everyone they knew had. A half-breed shifter witch was not welcome among purebred werewolves, but her brother Ambrose, Gunner's best friend, had changed that when he took over, hadn't he? At least for this one pack he had. Gunner had never worried about any of that as she was just Noelle to him.

He closed his eyes against visions of the past that clawed to the surface of his mind and realized his brother was still talking. "Bro, hotties heading our way. It's too late to fix you now." This time when Asher shoved, Gunner moved as his eyes flew open. Just a step closer to her but it was as if he jumped a chasm.

Noelle sauntered toward him, her friend in tow. A sweet smile spread across her pouty pink lips. A knowing smile. Gunner steeled himself against its impact. He knew this would come when he made the choice to return home. He just wasn't ready to see her tonight or for her to see him. But those lips brought a flash he'd give anything to forget, just to relieve the torture.

An image of her broke through, unbidden, from the past. That same smile as she sat waiting for him in the passenger seat of his Camaro on another winter night, reaching for something other than the gear shift, or at least not the one that belonged in his car.

"Gunner, fancy seeing you here." Noelle's silken voice pulled him out of the past.

"You're brother's invite clearly stated that I didn't have a choice."

Noelle smiled at the growl in his voice, clearly finding some kind of perverse pleasure in his words.

Asher glanced from Gunner to Noelle. "Dude, you know her?"

IS CONTEMPORARY MORE YOUR SPEED?

CHECK OUT THE INK & BRAZEN WOMEN SERIES
BY CASSIE LEIGH

Skin Deep
Available now from Sassy Typewriter Press

Mr. Right Now is planning on forever...
Gigi Duval doesn't do relationships, especially with her heart and career on the line. She values two things—her image and a good time in the bedroom. Watching men lie and cheat her whole life hardened her against "happily ever after". When she interviews with Roman Bishop, the sexy co-owner of Ink Spinners Tattoo, she begins to wonder if he might be more than a casual fling. Only one thing is certain: Roman is off limits. Gigi can't possibly add her best friend's brother to her little pink book. Or can she?

Turn the page for a sneak peek.

Roman's pencil tip dug into the front desk. His mind forced back from the memory he'd been drifting in as Declan Stone, his best friend and fellow artist, yanked the sketchpad away. Roman made an ineffectual grab for the spiral bound paper.

"What the hell, man?"

Declan leaned back in his chair, holding the artwork just out of reach. "Just checking out what you're doin'." He tossed the book down in front of Roman and pointed at the pinup girl meticulously drawn from memory on the page. "You've been spaced out since that chick last night."

"Yeah, so what?"

"So forget about it. She left with somebody else."

His friend was right. She did leave, but something about that look on her face as she had—as if she resigned herself to it but really wasn't interested. A woman like her could have anyone, which left him wondering why she'd gone, instead of telling the douche canoe to fuck off. Ultimately, it wasn't his place to get involved. In the rare down time he had between clients, he had better things to do than moon over the one who got away—like keeping the doors to their shop open.

Ink Spinners Tattoo & Gallery had been a dream and a labor of love for both Roman and Declan—one whose timetable moved up thanks to Roman's ex. The old brick building was one of the last the NewBo District had saved. They closed on the purchase just one week before the wrecking ball and saved it from becoming a new urban development made to look vintage. Thanks to the local historical society, they got it for a song and spent the better part of the year renovating it. Now the shop looked as if a steampunk barbershop and a

Victorian apothecary had a baby. For a couple of black sheep local boys, they were doing all right.

Roman dragged his hand over the rough stubble of his jaw. "You're right. Not like I could find her if I wanted to."

"Funny you should say that." A cocky grin split Declan's face just as the bell over the door rang.

Roman turned, smile at the ready as the girl in question sauntered through the door. "Damn."

Her steps faltered at his whispered oath, but he couldn't help himself. Ten seconds ago, he had no hope of ever seeing her again, let alone in his shop. Good girls like her don't have ink. Everything about her whispered that he was right, especially the way she dressed today; a blush pink blazer, layered over a white t-shirt that she tucked into a pink and black rose patterned pencil skirt. She had tamed the dark curls he remembered from last night into a bun, and oversized pearl earrings hung from earlobes that he already visualized sucking on.

"You're Ann's step-brother?" Her voice held the same breathless wonder that he uttered his own curse in seconds before. When she continued, her tone was brighter, with crisp efficiency. "I'm here about the job. Ann Kennedy referred me."

The attitude switch about gave him whiplash.

She held out her hand and as he stood to take it, her soft, slender fingers seemed swallowed up by his darker, tattooed mitt. "Roman Bishop and this is my business partner, Declan Stone, you are…"

"Oh yeah, I'm Gigi Duval." She stared up into his eyes, leaving her hand in his for longer than necessary before she seemed to notice and pull back.

He forced down a groan at the simple loss of her warmth

in his hand. She wet her pouty pink lips. When his gaze zeroed in on the subtle movement, the corners turned up, ever so slightly. This couldn't be good. Mere moments into formally meeting her and he was already smitten. Would it be strange to propose marriage now? Oh wait—she had a boyfriend—at least she did last night.

***

Gigi would give anything to rollback her day to lunch and hand that card back to Ann or better yet, keep the card and refuse to give that forced promise. Life could be an unforgiving bitch and right now, life clearly had it in for Gigi. Why did it have to be him?

There was no one in the history of man that made a plain white t-shirt and jeans look that good—except maybe James Dean. Roman's clothes weren't plain. They were a statement. A white wall, allowing the brilliant color and bold black lines of ink running up both arms to speak for him. Her panties were insta-soaked just imagining tracing each intricate design with her tongue. Add to that, the amber fire of his eyes, he was just too much. Roman Bishop was the worst kind of temptation.

If she hoped to keep that ill-fated vow, let alone her precious rules, she would need to turn tail and run back the way she came. Unfortunately, her fat mouth must be under the sway of her hormones or her dwindling bank account.

"Ann said you need an office manager. So here I am, resume in hand." She whipped out a crisp sheet of paper from her folder as evidence. He took it without even glancing at the words. "Has the position been filled?"

"You're hired." His voice held a note of awe and his eyes seemed to spark.

"I'm sorry? Aren't you going to interview me?" She raised one eyebrow as she looked from Roman to Declan, who stood chuckling beside him.

He leaned forward across the desk, his fingers gripping the edge, turning his knuckles white. "If you couldn't do the job, Ann wouldn't have sent you. You need a job. I have one to fill. What more do I need to know?"

about the author

CASSIE LEIGH writes contemporary and paranormal romance that is more than skin deep. Before she could write, she began dreaming up stories. Cassie has since moved on from recorded conversations for her dolls on a Fisher-Price cassette player, to novels that draw on her plethora of eccentric passions including Monsters, MMA fighting and Pinup style. Every new obsession seems to find its way into her romance world! She aspires to create character driven drama that have nothing to do with reality. Want more? You can connect with Cassie Leigh online.

https://www.facebook.com/cassieleighauthor
https://www.twitter.com/cassieleigh322
https://www.amazon.com/author/leighcassie

To get the inside track on all new releases, sign up for her newsletter on her web site at
https://www.cassieleighauthor.com

by cassie leigh

Haunted Romance Series
Until Death Do Us Part
Follow You Anywhere
Redeem My Broken Soul (coming soon)

Ushers Run Pack
Home For The Howliday

Ink & Brazen Women
Skin Deep
Business Casual (available in the Seduction In A Suit anthology)
Leading Man (coming soon)
How About Never (coming soon)

THE CROWN

A Dark Fairy Tale

GENEVIEVE RAAS

Ravenwell Press

Ravenwell Press Paperback ISBN: 978-1-944912-18-5
eBook ISBN: 978-1-944912-12-3

First Edition